PENGUIN BOOKS

RIVER OF DOLLS AND OTHER STORIES

American Suzanne Kamata has lived in Japan for over thirty years. Her writing has appeared in *The Best Asian Short Stories* in 2017, 2022, and 2023 and *The Best Asian Travel Writing 2020, The APWT Drunken Boat Anthology of New Writing, Telltale Food: Writings from the Fay Khoo Award 2017–2019*, and numerous other anthologies. She is the author of a previous short story collection, *The Beautiful One Has Come* (2011), which won a Nautilus Silver Award and a Next Generation Indie Best Award; the young adult novels *Gadget Girl: The Art of Being Invisible* (2013), named an Honor Book by the Asian American Pacific Librarians Association, and *Indigo Girl* (2019) a Freeman Honor Book. Her most recent novel is *The Baseball Widow* (2021). She is an associate professor at Naruto University of Education.

ADVANCE PRAISE FOR
RIVER OF DOLLS AND OTHER STORIES

'Kamata strikes the perfect balance of [the] bittersweet with the humorous—brilliant! These are stories for our times.'

—Simon Rowe, author of
Mami Suzuki: Private Eye

'Suzanne Kamata's narratives flow like sonatas. She writes about life lived across oceans, bringing together multiple flavours of varied cultures with a soupçon of humour, poignancy, and vibrancy. I would not want to miss any book by her!'

—Mitali Chakravarty, editor and founder
of *Borderless Journal*, and author
of *Flight of the Angsana Oriole*

'Kamata is a dazzling, deeply empathetic writer.'

—Kevin Chong, author of
The Double Life of Benson Yu

River of Dolls and Other Stories

Suzanne Kamata

PENGUIN BOOKS
An imprint of Penguin Random House

PENGUIN BOOKS

Penguin Books is an imprint of the Penguin Random House group of companies whose addresses can be found at global.penguinrandomhouse.com

Published by Penguin Random House SEA Pte Ltd
40 Penjuru Lane, #03-12, Block 2
Singapore 609216

First published in Penguin Books by Penguin Random House SEA 2024

10 9 8 7 6 5 4 3 2 1

ISBN 9789815204964

Typeset in Adobe Caslon Pro by MAP Systems, Bengaluru, India

For Meredith and Susan
with thanks for all your support

Contents

Day Pass

1

France

17

Blue Murder

25

The Incan Ice Maiden

37

Love After 9/11

49

Down the Mountain

61

River of Dolls

69

Lessons
87

The Snow Woman
101

A Real Job
115

Julia in the Desert
125

The Woman Who Loved Insects
139

The Lump
151

Mon-chan
159

Peace on Earth
171

Acknowledgements
185

Day Pass

Every time Savannah speaks, a thousand magnolias bloom in my head. Her voice is liquid and sweet, like honey drizzled in the ear. There is none of the redneck twang that fills up the pool halls and Laundromats. Her voice is worth imitating, and as I drive home after my shift at the restaurant, the smell of grease clinging to my hair and polyester, I sugar my syllables and speak into the night.

Savannah doesn't look like a prisoner. I don't know what wrong thing she did to land in the Women's Correctional Institute outside of town, only that she goes there after work when her apron is plumped and padded with dollar bills. I've never asked her and she's never told me. Savannah—with her Snow White colouring, her pale, translucent skin stretched tight over delicate bones—would have made a good nineteenth-century invalid in a lacy Victorian gown. She wouldn't look out of place in hoopskirts on the porch of one of those plantation mansions I visited when I first arrived in South Carolina two years ago. I came from Michigan with my college scholarship and a trunk of new clothes.

I've decided that I will make Savannah my project. Something tells me that the two of us can be friends.

I work at the salad bar with Cora, a tall woman with a gold tooth and brown skin. She was arrested for writing bad cheques, but now she's out on parole. While we chop the lettuce and slice the tomatoes, she tells me about her new boyfriend.

'I like him fine,' she says, 'but I hate it when he sticks his tongue in my ear.'

Savannah walks by balancing a tray loaded with fried chicken dinners on one hand.

Cora lays down her knife on the chopping board and puts her hands on her hips. 'There goes Miss Hoity-Toity,' she says.

Anger coils in me like a snake. 'Why do you say that?' I try to keep the edge out of my voice.

'She don't talk to nobody!' Cora says. 'She think she's too good for us.'

'I think she's just reserved,' I say. 'Shy.' I have seen the way she bites her lip in worry, the way her gaze pulls back into her eyes when someone is rude. There are invisible walls around her, but she is no prima donna.

'Girl, you may be goin' to college, but you don't know nothin' about people,' Cora says, picking up the knife again.

Phyllis, another waitress who is behind us filling salt shakers, snickers. I glare at her, at her doughy flesh and dangling cigarette, but she doesn't notice.

From the very beginning, I've felt protective of Savannah, even though she is twenty-six, seven years older than me. We often take our dinner breaks together.

'What are you gonna be when you finish college?' she asks me one night while we are eating.

'An interpreter or an NPO worker,' I reply. 'I want to use my French and live in foreign countries.'

Her violet eyes fix on me and sparkle with interest. 'You mean like France? That sounds really exciting. I've never been outside of South Carolina, except for one time Mama and me went up to Graceland.'

Actually, I want to go to poor countries, places where I will be needed, where I can make a difference. At one time, I thought I would like to go to Rwanda to help Dian Fossey save the gorillas, but last year, after she was murdered, I changed my mind. I don't say this. I let Savannah fill her head with cafes and the Eiffel Tower. I imagine teaching her French and helping her win a scholarship to France.

Savannah doesn't speak in the language of my textbooks, but I know that isn't her fault. The lovely lilt of her voice, the grace of her movements when she lifts a glass to her lips suggest an innate elegance.

'What do you want to be?' I ask her.

Some of the waitresses have spent their entire working lives in food service. Carrying trays and sweet-talking customers is the only thing they know how to do, and they'll probably keep doing it till they're old enough to collect Social Security cheques. Savannah, I know, is not one of them. She is meant for something else.

Her eyes stray from my face, and her mind seems to drift past the time clock, past the leering cook who keeps smacking his lips at us as we eat, through the door, and out into another world.

'I want to be a secretary,' she finally says. 'I can type pretty fast.'

It's a modest dream, and I am touched by her simple aspirations. My friends and I wanted to be artists and astronauts, and then later, lawyers, teachers, and engineers. If I spend enough time with her, perhaps I can convince her to strive for more.

I am careful not to ask her about prison, but sometimes she volunteers information.

'We can go out on a day pass if someone checks us out. My mother comes once in a while and takes me to see a movie or something,' she says.

She picks the lettuce leaf and tomato off her hamburger and eats them. The rest of the food has grown cold on the plate. Her appetite, never good, seems especially bad tonight.

It's then that I get the idea to take her shopping. I figure she must have money if she has a job. I could help her feel normal for a while. I could give her freedom, if only for a few hours.

I feel the importance of my mission. I will be her saviour. I will be her guide for virtuous living. I am momentarily entranced by an image of us having lunch together downtown, double-dating, going to the movies. We'll be like sisters, trading secrets and make-up tips, laughing together.

'When is your next day off?' I ask her.

Columbia Women's Correctional Institute is out in the middle of a field, off the highway. The prison is a minimum-security facility, and there is no need for barbed wire fences or high-strung dogs.

I park my battered Volkswagen Beetle in the gravel lot and a security guard ambles over. He has a gun in the holster strapped to his waist. Suspicion flickers in his dark eyes.

'I'm gonna have to ask you to open the trunk, ma'am,' he says.

I get out, stick the key in the lock, and step back to let him carry out his inspection. Although I know it's just routine, I am excited by the procedure. Most people take one look at my blue eyes and blonde hair and lump me in with the good girls. At the back of my high school yearbooks, classmates always wrote things like 'to one of the nicest people I've ever met' or 'stay sweet'. So when this husky cop lifts the spare tire for a look underneath and feels along the lining of the trunk, I can't help but feel flattered. This man thinks I might be dangerous—a gangster's moll, a conveyor of contraband, a spy.

He noses around in the back seat, the glove box, under the mats. Finally, he turns to me with a look of apology. 'Okay. Thanks. You can go in now.'

I nod, affecting disdain, then stride away with my head held high.

I push through the front door and find myself in a waiting room. I go up to the window on the left wall and say, 'I've come for Savannah Powers.' It's like checking in at the doctor's office.

The woman on the other side hands me a sheaf of papers. I fill out each one, writing my name, address, phone number, and place of employment. Then, I pass the papers back through the window, and Savannah appears.

'Hey,' I say.

'Hey.' It's the first time I've seen her in regular clothes. She's wearing a denim mini-skirt that doesn't do much for her skinny legs and a black short-sleeved shirt shot through with gold threads.

'Are you ready to go?' I ask.

She nods and her lips curve into a sweet smile.

I'm filled with a sense of well-being.

'Be back by five,' the woman at the desk says calmly.

I take her to the mall and we walk around, running our fingers over the clothes on the racks, browsing in gift shops full of knick-knacks and paperweights. I watch her delicate hands as she picks up a small ceramic poodle and examines it, rolling it around on her palm. I watch until she puts it back on the shelf, then look away, feeling ashamed for not trusting her.

As far as I know, she is not a thief. I imagine she was more of a victim. Perhaps she fell in with a rough crowd. Maybe she had to go against her principles just to survive.

There is an air of melancholy about her as we wander past the Orange Julius, the Waldenbooks, the video arcade. I'm thinking that it's a longing to be free to buy the clothes she sees draped in the windows and then wear them out dancing and to restaurants or a wish that the simple pleasure of window shopping was something that she could indulge in every day.

Neither one of us buys anything. We walk back to the car slowly and settle into the sun-warmed vinyl seats.

'I came here to die once,' Savannah says quietly.

It takes a moment for the words to register, and even then, I think I must be mistaken.

'What?'

'I swallowed a bunch of pills and I wandered around the mall until I collapsed. Somebody called an ambulance.'

I stare at the steering wheel for a long time, concentrating on the rubber grooves my fingers fit into. 'I'm sorry' is the only thing I can think of saying. I'm not sure if she has heard me. When I turn to look at her again, she is staring wistfully at the sprawling building.

I start the engine but realize that we have no destination. The day stretches before us like a desert of minutes.

'Where do you want to have lunch?' I ask her. It's not quite noon, but my stomach is grumbling.

'Let's go to Krystal's.'

Her choice surprises me, but I try not to show it. The burgers there are tiny and the buns taste like wet cardboard. After what I imagine she eats in prison, it seems like she'd want something a little more gourmet, but for all I know, she likes the place. Or maybe it's a question of money. Maybe she's got less to spend than I think. I consider her birdlike frame and her eating habits, and I realize that food probably isn't a big priority for her.

We order our burgers and fries and get a table by the window. The place is already filling up. At another table, there's a plump couple in shorts and T-shirts tight enough to reveal the rolls of flesh underneath. Across from us is a harried-looking woman with spongy pink rollers in her hair and a baby with a ketchup-smeared face sitting on her lap. Then there's a gangly teenager with long scraggly hair, a gold stud glinting in her earlobe, and a T-shirt with the name of some obscure band printed on it. Savannah seems oblivious to the clientele. She eats slowly and primly, staring out at the parking lot.

I'm about midway through my fries when she pushes the remains of her lunch aside and says, 'I want to call a friend of mine. Do you mind? I'll be right back.'

I nod. I'm not her warden, after all.

She removes herself from the table and pushes through the wheezing doors. There isn't a phone booth in sight. Maybe there's one behind the building. I continue eating. The day is not going as well as I'd imagined. We've already exhausted small talk during our dinner breaks at work and digging deeper seems risky. I realize that Savannah has many secrets, many hidden sorrows. What does she want to do, I wonder. What would cheer her up? Should we go to the zoo? An amusement park? A movie? For the rest of the day, I'll let her call the shots. I eat the remaining fries one by one. I eat my little burgers.

I eat the burgers that Savannah ordered and left, unwrapped and uneaten. She's still not back when I finish my meal, so I order a Styrofoam cup of coffee, then take the steaming brew back to the table and sip it slowly. I'm on my second cup when I look at my watch and discover half an hour has gone by and Savannah's not back yet. I stuff the wrappings of lunch into a trash can and go outside to look for her. There's a phone booth at the side of the restaurant, but she's not in it. I circle the building. I can't find her. She's gone.

Savannah could be miles away by now, in a friend's car, laughing and smiling. Anger flares up and quickly fizzles away. I feel disappointment and shame more than anything else. I trusted her. I thought we were friends. Tears burn behind my eyes, but I grit my teeth and will them not to fall. I sit down on the curb and pound my knees with my fists.

And then she appears, coming from around the corner of the hamburger shop. She's smiling sweetly, walking with a loping springy step. We get into the car as if nothing has happened. She is breathing heavily with her lips parted. I catch a whiff of mint chewing gum, and under that, something I can't quite identify. The Party Town Liquor Store across the street catches my eye. I study Savannah, but I can't be sure that she's done anything wrong.

'So, where to next?' I ask her, deciding to ignore the last forty minutes.

'Let's go to my house.'

I nod. 'Okay. Tell me how to get there.'

We pull into the heavy noon traffic and she gives directions.

'My mother will like you,' she assures me. 'She'll be happy that I have a friend like you.'

I expect her mother to be a chain-smoking, heavily mascaraed trailer park queen. I figure that she's a beer-drinking, belching, man-loving broad, too busy with sex and sin to raise her daughter right. When she comes to the door to greet us, I meet a soft-spoken woman with gently permed brown hair. There is no make-up to hide the dark circles under her eyes or fill in the creases on her forehead. She's wearing a house dress.

'Come in, come in,' she says with lowered eyes. She plumps her hair with one hand and waves us in with the other. She makes a show of straightening the magazines and newspapers that are strewn about and shoos away a cat so that I can sit down.

'This is Amelia,' Savannah says, introducing me. 'She goes to USC. She's going to be an interpreter.'

Her mother smiles warmly and reaches out her hand. 'So nice to meet you.'

'Nice to meet you too.' I take her hand. It's warm. Her grip is firm.

It occurs to me that Savannah is using me as a cover. She can bring me here as evidence that she is on the straight and narrow, and the next time she gets into trouble, her mother will sob and wring her tear-soaked handkerchief saying, 'I don't understand. She was such a good girl.'

I realize that while my Goldilocks exterior hides nothing, Savannah is capable of duality.

Her mother brings us sweetened ice tea and begins updating her daughter on family news—a cousin's marriage, someone else's promotion. While the two of them talk, I take in my surroundings. There's a bowling trophy on top of the television, 'Home Sweet Home' in cross stitch on the wall. There is nothing in this room, with its doilies and coasters and flowered curtains, to explain Savannah's bad behaviour. It's not so different from the house where I grew up.

Finally, Savannah sets her drained glass on a low table and says, 'I know. Let's go to the park in front of the Capitol.'

I'm relieved by her suggestion. I've enjoyed many lazy afternoons strolling among the statues and feeding squirrels. At least we have one pleasure in common, I think, as we say 'goodbye' to her mom and get back into the car.

We buy a bag of peanuts at a nearby newsstand, then settle on a bench at the edge of the luxuriant green lawn. One by one the grey squirrels approach us, flicking their bushy tails. Soon we are surrounded on all sides by curious and hungry creatures. The music of Savannah's laughter rings through the air.

'They're so greedy!' she says, fishing for a peanut. She is light and girlish for the first time today. I watch as a squirrel snatches a nut from her slender fingers and scurries off.

Then she turns to me and says, 'When I was a kid, me and my friend used to dress up in old clothes and pretend we were homeless.' Her honeyed voice is conspiratorial with a hint of mischief.

'Oh?' It's not a game that would have occurred to me as a child. My companions and I liked to imitate Mary Poppins.

'We used to come here and beg for money,' she continues. 'One time a man came and took us out to eat. We didn't want the food, though. We wanted the money.' She laughs at the memory.

I laugh with her, but my laughter is forced and edgy. I look at her bone-china face and her fairy-tale features and think how she'd once sat in this very same park in torn, dirty clothes, *hustling*. I'm beginning to think that she was not led astray, that badness was something she came into on her own.

'We'd better go back now,' I say, glancing at my watch. 'I wouldn't want you to get into trouble.' We have time to spare, but I am weary from the surprises of the day. I'm also beginning to wonder if she might be trying to hustle *me*. I need to take control of this situation.

In the car, with my eyes on the highway, I finally ask the question that has been at the back of my mind since I met her. 'What did you do to get into prison?'

There is the slightest pause before she replies and I feel a moment of guilt. It's none of my business, after all.

But she answers, and her voice is clear and strong.

'I was dating this crazy guy—Eddie, was his name. We had some wild times, let me tell you. Anyway, we were smokin' and talkin' one night and we got this idea to rob a motel down at Myrtle Beach. Eddie had a gun and he can be pretty scary if he wants to be.'

My fingers tighten on the steering wheel. Somehow, I was imagining something tamer, like Cora's bad cheques.

Savannah continues her story. 'So we drove down there, smokin' and drinkin' all the way, and we picked out this fleabag motel. Eddie kept saying, "No, no. We should do the Sheraton. They got more money there." But I told him that was a bad idea. All them bell boys and valets—someone'd be bound to see us. We went to the Surfside Motel, I believe that's what it was called, and we entered the office. It was late, so nobody was checking in or out. Everybody had passed out or gone to bed.'

Could she be making all of this up? I glance over at her. She's gazing off into the distance, as if lost in memory. If she were lying, wouldn't she be checking my reaction?

'The motel clerk, he was this kinda fat guy with glasses, about forty years old, not much hair on his head. The TV was on and he was slouched down in a chair, asleep. He was sleeping on the job!' Savannah snorts in disbelief. 'Eddie said, "This'll be easy," but the guy started wakin' up. While he was twisting around and smacking his lips, Eddie got ready. The guy opened his eyes and saw a gun pointed right in his face. Suddenly he was wide awake and screamin' like a mad man. "Don't shoot me! I don't wanna die. Please. I got a wife and kids."'

I'm not sure I like where this story is going, but I can't figure out how to stop her. I keep my eyes on the road ahead.

Savannah pauses and licks her lips. 'Eddie said, like a cool dude, "Just give us the money and we won't hurt a hair on your head." And then we cracked up laughing because he hadn't got but a few hairs on that big ol' head of his.'

I force a laugh. It's more of a bark.

'He got out of the chair a little too quickly,' Savannah continues. 'Eddie said, "Whoa there, buddy. Put your hands over your head where I can see them and move slowly."

'Just when he reached the cash register, we heard a siren off in the distance and Eddie started to get nervous. "Y'know, Savannah, maybe this isn't such a good idea," he said. He lowered the gun, and I swear that clerk looked like he was about ready to throw a party, he was so happy.'

I suddenly feel happy for this guy. The air whooshes from my lungs and my shoulders loosen. But then Savannah cackles, and her story goes on.

'So I said, "Gimme that gun!" and I grabbed it away from Eddie and aimed it at the fool behind the cash register. "Open it now," I said, "or I'll blow your head off."'

Oh. My. God.

'He kinda whimpered, like a puppy, and I smelled something funny. I moved in closer and looked over the counter. There was this big wet spot spreading across the front of his pants. *He'd peed his pants.* It was running over his shiny black shoes and onto the floor.'

Poor guy. I feel dizzy and I wonder if she is planning to do something to me. Should I pull the car over and tell her to scram? Or maybe it's better just to stay calm. I take a deep breath and let her keep talking. In spite of myself, I want to hear how everything turns out.

'"I'm gonna count to ten," I said. He started hurrying up then. By the time he got the drawer open he was crying and his tears were falling on the money. Eddie went around and cleared out the drawer. There was hardly any money in there. "Where's the rest?" I asked him. He mumbled something about credit cards. I was thinking that there must be a safe in the joint, but Eddie said, "Forget it. Let's just go." We yanked the phone cord and hightailed it out of there.'

When Savannah finishes her story, her cheeks are flushed, and her eyes are diamond-bright. She looks at me for a reaction. All I can say is, 'Wow.' What I'm thinking is: *She had a gun. She could have killed someone.* Yet, even after all I've heard, she still has a pull on me, like the moon on water. There is that voice, that almost transparent skin, and maybe something else, something at the heart of me that loves darkness and danger.

For a split second, I could go either way. I see myself trailing after her into a 7-Eleven at midnight, a stocking over my face. I picture us in the getaway car and my foot presses down harder on the gas pedal.

And then I imagine myself getting caught. Getting arrested. Losing my job. Getting kicked out of school. And somehow, I see myself locked up, alone, and Savannah on the outside, laughing.

Who was I kidding? She's not going to fall under my good-girl spell. In some ways she's probably smarter than I am. Street smart. It occurs to me that I was wrong about her; she's not Snow White. Maybe she's wearing a beautiful disguise. Maybe she's more like the old woman offering a poisoned apple.

Back at the prison, I escort her inside. A lady guard appears to lead her back to her room. My first impulse is to turn and run back to my car without a backward glance. But Savannah reaches to me and gives me a hug. 'Thank you,' she says. This embrace is so unexpected that I wonder if it's for the sake of the guard who hovers nearby, watching every move we make.

'I had a great time,' she says.

I don't say anything, not even goodbye.

It isn't until the guard touches her elbow that I realize I've been holding my breath. I don't exhale until Savannah is beyond the door and I know she can't get out.

France

Le Style

There are certain things a French woman would never do. For instance, she would never ever wear jogging shoes with a business suit. A French woman would suffer for fashion and walk kilometres and kilometres in three-inch spikes if need be, and she wouldn't whimper. She wouldn't say a word.

An American woman, incongruously dressed in designer pinstripes and rubber-soled sports shoes, would gaze at the French woman with reverential awe. She would immediately recognize the superior style of her European sister, and while she would praise herself for her good sense, she would also feel hopelessly frumpy. Some things are more important than convenience and comfort. Sacrifices must be made.

I sit in my bed for hours with the curtains drawn around me like white cotton veils, studying the French fashion magazines that the nurse brings me. I give the nurse money and she goes out into the 'real' world to bring me back images of what she calls the 'fantasy world'.

'The world is what you make of it,' I say quietly.

She looks back at me—me, this pale, thin woman with unwashed hair—and says, 'Ain't that the truth?'

I have been keeping a list of things that I will buy when I get out of the hospital. The mannequins are always wearing big hoops hooked to their ears and brilliantly coloured scarves over their heads, around their necks, bandeau-style across their bosoms. Their eyes are often smudged with black liner and cigarettes dangle from their pouty lips. They always look like they just got out of bed, and they can't wait to dive back under the covers as soon as the photographer is finished. They wear tight, tight jeans, fuzzy sweaters, and leather skirts. When I leave this place I will buy the earrings, the scarves, the jeans, the sweaters, the skirts, and the cigarettes. One day I will be more French than Vanessa Paradis.

'How would you describe yourself?' Dr Smith asks. He always throws out these essay questions during our afternoon sessions. (What was your relationship with your mother? Do you have recurring dreams? How do you feel when you see a naked person?)

I pretend not to hear and look out the window, pick up the paperweight on his desk and set it back down, then bite my fingernails.

'How would you describe yourself?'

'I am a blob,' I say.

He tries not to betray his disappointment, but I catch a quick flash of impatience. His pen rests against his hand.

I try again. 'I am a blob seeking style and substance.'

He likes this better and nods, as if he were identifying a disease from a textbook. He makes a note on the pad in front of him, which is always angled away from me.

I seem to have made some progress.

La Cuisine

William took me to a French restaurant on our first date. It was called Chez Pierre and it was in a shopping centre along with a Laundromat and a butcher. Walking through the door, I was like Alice going through her looking glass. The storefront was entirely at odds with the opulence inside. The draperies covering the wall looked as though they had been snatched out of Louis XVI's living room. The waiters were tall, thin, and elegant.

William ordered the food in flawless French. He was part of the scenery while I wondered what to do with all those forks. A few minutes later, the waiter appeared with a bottle of wine. William glanced at the label, smelled the cork, swirled the wine in his glass, tasted, and proclaimed, 'Excellent.'

I was stunned by his savoir faire. I melted and oozed over the table, absolutely enamoured. William. Guillaume. I loved him already.

First, we sampled escargot bathed in butter. Next came a flaky white fish that had been poached in wine, then filet of beef with truffles. Then salad, followed by delicate layers of pastry plumped with cream. We drank wine, coffee, cognac.

In the hospital, the food is always bland and monochromatic as if seasonings and spices would excite the patients too much.

La Passion

One day I took all the plates out of the cupboard and smashed them. I threw them against the walls, against the floor, against the ceiling. When William came home from work, he was probably expecting the aroma of dinner and my arms around his neck. Instead, he found me sitting in a pile of shards, my fingers bleeding. He didn't say a word to me. He went into the other room and whipped out his phone.

In French movies, women have visions, they scream, try to kill their lovers, chop off their hair. The French recognize obsession as a mark of passion. They are obsessed with obsession.

If I were French, William would have picked me up out of the refuse and taken me to bed to ravish me. Instead, he called the hospital.

L'Amour

There is a man who comes once a week to visit his wife. I am in love with him. I have met his wife, a very nervous woman. If they let her out, she would try to kill herself, so they keep her here and feed her scrambled eggs. She has wispy hair and I suspect that her husband is no longer in love with her, and maybe it's her money he's spending and that's why he must visit. Her husband is unfaithful to her. He has a mistress. Me.

I used to watch him from the shadows. When he took his wife out to the yard for air I hid behind a tree, hovering, waiting for the right moment. I watched him smooth her hair back as if she were an old woman and hold her hand as if she were a young child at a street crossing.

She is fat from the drugs and the starchy food, though she might have been beautiful at one time.

Her husband and I make love in the broom closet, stumbling over a bucket of soapy mop water. I don't wear panties on the days he comes. He lifts up my nightgown and murmurs '*Ma cherie, ma cherie.*'

Le Parfum

Sometimes William comes to see me. I know it's because he feels guilty about the damage he's done to my life. He never stays long and he spends his visits shifting from one foot to another and dipping his hands in and out of his pockets. He brings me presents. They are presents for a sick person—nightgowns, books of crossword puzzles, potted plants. Except once he brought me a bottle of Chanel No. 5.

If the nurse comes into my room while he's there, he complains to her about me. 'Why won't she talk to me?' he asks. 'She just ignores me.'

The nurse chuckles. 'Well, sometimes she pretends she can't speak English. Pretends she's French.'

Then William says softly, '*Bonjour. Ça va?*'

I sigh and turn to the window. He doesn't understand that I want him to leave.

I usually give his presents away or throw them in the bin. The only thing I wanted to keep was the perfume. The nurse took it away from me, though. I heard her tell another nurse that she was afraid I'd drink it or break the bottle and cut myself.

The next day when she walked into the room, I could smell the delicate, expensive scent emanating from the crook of her arm.

L'Art

Three times a week we make things. Now we are making ashtrays, although I don't know anyone who smokes. I figure I will glaze mine a boudoir pink and keep bobby pins and paper clips in it. This is supposed to make us feel like artists, but anyone can press their thumbs into clay forming indentations that will cradle ash.

One patient has modelled ten ashtrays. We think that she can sell them on eBay. They are very vivid, with colours that crazy people like—yellow, orange, red, sometimes black.

Before the ashtrays, we made birdhouses. Pounding nails was supposed to unleash our fury. I didn't put a door on mine because I believe that birds aren't meant to live in a miniature split-level A-frame chalet. Birds need to make things too. I explained this to the nurse, but she told me to make a door anyway. Afterwards, I smashed the house with my hammer.

In our afternoon session, the doctor asked me about this. 'Why did you destroy your birdhouse? Were you dissatisfied with your work?'

'Birds aren't like people,' I said. 'They don't need houses.' I told him that I wanted to paint pictures.

'What kind of pictures would you like to paint?' he asked me.

'I like Expressionism.'

I think of *The Scream* by Edvard Munch. It is not the kind of painting you'd find here. The doctors and nurses have hung Norman Rockwell prints on the wall so that we can see what normal looks like. In Munch's painting, there is an emaciated man holding his head as if it may fall off, his mouth forever open as he screams a silent eternal scream. No one can hear him. Except for me.

Sometimes I look into the mirror, hold my head, open my mouth, and scream. Then right away, I pick up my sketch pad and pencil and I draw myself screaming.

Les Avenues

I am walking down a long avenue lined with trees. Beyond the trees, there are fields of wheat. I am thinking of another wide avenue lined with exclusive boutiques and cafes. On holidays, presidents parade down this street, followed by soldiers on horses. On ordinary days, like this one, women dressed in all black stroll along the sidewalk with their chic, ugly little dogs. At the end, there is a huge stone arch. I've seen it in picture books and on postcards. I've never seen it in person, but I'll recognize it right away.

In a few hours the nurses will start looking for me. They will call William and maybe the police. My picture will be in the newspaper and they'll say I escaped, that I may be dangerous. But I don't care. I am on my way to Paris. I will call my lover and he will leave his wispy-haired wife for good. We will go to the City of Lights. I've never been there, but I know I will like it. It'll be like heaven.

Blue Murder

On the first day of spring, Keita Hosokawa fell in love with a bird. If anyone had told him a week before that this would happen, he wouldn't have believed it. He was fed up of birds. Specifically crows.

That year, the crows seemed greater in number than ever before. Fatter too. They feasted at the roadside shrines where humpbacked ladies set out oranges and bowls of cooked rice for their dear departed. They swooped down on cemeteries and ate the offerings from gravestones. They ate until they were as big as roosters, until it seemed as if the telephone wires would not support them.

As if there wasn't enough food available elsewhere, they fed in Keita's orchard. He could see them from the window as he ate his breakfast—a murder of crows settling in the branches of his pear trees. The sight of them made him weary before the day's work had even begun. He turned away from the window and tried to smile at his son.

Ichiro sat in his high chair, banging his spoon on the tray. His bib was soaked with drool. 'Wan wan wan!' he said, barking like a dog.

Keita sighed. He tried to get the boy to say '*otosan*' or even 'papa', which was easier to pronounce than the Japanese word for father, but he wouldn't learn. He could say 'mama' and make a variety of animal sounds, but he seemed to wilfully ignore Keita.

'Papa,' Keita said softly, trying once again.

Ichiro's spoon flew out of his spit-slimed hand and onto the floor. 'Miaow,' he said, spotting Kitty in the corner.

'Papa,' Keita repeated.

From the kitchen, his wife, Misa, giggled. 'Don't feel so bad,' she said. 'He doesn't see you enough to know who you are. He'll figure it out soon enough.'

'He doesn't see me because I'm out in the field trying to protect his legacy,' Keita said, suddenly feeling angry. He knew that Ichiro wasn't to blame. He was a baby. He slept almost all of the time. When he was a little bigger, Keita would take him out into the orchard and prop him against a tree. 'This is all yours,' he would tell him as his own father had once taught him. 'Someday you'll take care of these trees.'

Even if Keita and Misa had other children, Ichiro, as the firstborn son, was entitled to the family property. The land with all of the trees and the house would be passed on just as it had been for generations before.

Normally, Keita's parents were at the breakfast table with them, but they had departed the previous day for Texas to visit Keita's sister. She was a doctor, and she had gone to the United States to do research and learn the latest treatments for kidney diseases. Keita's parents worried about her because she was past thirty and as yet unmarried. It didn't matter to them that she had bought her own house and drove in an imported car or that she could afford annual vacations to Europe. They had hopes of a traditional life for her—one with a husband and kids. Still, she was allowed to do as she pleased. Keita, as the oldest son, was the one who was bound to follow their desires.

When Keita had turned twenty-nine, his mother had declared that it was time for him to take a bride. He felt the weight of duty and meekly agreed. His first choice of wife, a shy young woman with waist-length hair and dimples, seemed to like him but refused the role of a farm wife. The next ten women he met had virtually identical reactions. They wanted to have careers in tall, air-conditioned buildings. They didn't want to share the roof with his parents. He was thinking that he might have to settle for a foreign bride, one of the Southeast Asians sent to Japan to marry the country's undesirable bachelors, and he wondered how he would be able to communicate with such a woman. He had never studied Thai or Tagalog, and his English wasn't very good.

But then his luck had changed. A family friend introduced him to Misa, a woman who had grown up on a farm. She knew all about pears—how to pollinate them, how to batten the low branches when a typhoon was approaching, how to turn them into a sweet liqueur. Her hair was short, and she didn't mind getting dirt under her fingernails.

The mayor had attended the wedding and made a speech praising their complementary qualities. Keita had always been a dreamy boy, he said, but Misa was of simple tastes and practical, and she would keep him tethered to the earth. They honeymooned in Hawaii, where Keita marvelled at the acres of pineapples and sugar cane. What it must be like to be in charge of all that! His family's farm was modest in comparison.

For the first year of their marriage, Keita and Misa had worked side by side among the trees, but then she became pregnant, and nausea and headaches had forced her to stay in the house.

On this day, Keita would be going into the field alone. Misa would play with Ichiro. Maybe she'd watch the afternoon dramas while he napped. With Keita's mother in Texas, she'd be able to relax for a change. Keita too. The bickering women made him feel tired, made him almost want to stay in the orchard.

He scraped the last grain of rice from his bowl and pushed the breakfast dishes away. 'I guess I'd better get out there before the crows eat all of my fruit.'

Misa murmured her agreement and then gathered up the dishes for washing.

Ichiro said, 'Moo!'

He could hear the crows as he stomped onto the field in his work boots. 'Kah! Kah!' They seemed to be mocking him, telling jokes at his expense.

Keita didn't know how to make them go away. He'd staked up a scarecrow—a straw man in a floppy hat, plaid shirt, and worn-out jeans—at the centre of the field, but the birds didn't seem to mind. They perched on the dummy's shoulder. He'd then tied aluminium pie pans to the branches of trees, having heard that the metallic brilliance would ward off feathered intruders, but after a day or two of being wary, the crows had returned in full force.

If he'd had a gun, he would have blasted into the trees, but he had no such weapon. A sudden burst of fury sparked him with energy. He filled his lungs and screamed, 'Iiiiiiyyaaaa!' He ran through the orchard waving his arms like a madman. The crows lifted into the air, flecking the sky with black. They circled cautiously, then one brave bird descended towards the trees again.

Keita sighed. If it wasn't crows, it was typhoons. If it wasn't weather, it was blight. He wished that he could take one season off from farming. A few months in, say, an office would refresh him.

He had been to the doctor recently to find out why he was always so tired. His body felt worn and damaged even though he was just thirty years old. His eyesight was failing, his girth expanding, his intestinal tract rebelling after every meal.

'Too much stress,' the doctor told him. 'You'll have to stop smoking and drinking, and you'd better find another job.'

Keita had laughed. If only it were that simple. He had signed up for a karate class—he'd reached black belt while in college—hoping for physical release. But the weekly sparring matches left him breathless and sore, and he found himself being defeated by sixteen-year-old beginners.

Now, standing in the field, he thought about all the work that had to be done. He knew that he could call on the neighbouring farmers to help, since his parents were out of the country, but asking them seemed like too much trouble. All he wanted to do was lie down under the trees and sleep.

Instead, he scrabbled for a stone and tossed it up at a plump black bird. 'Kah!' The crow ruffled its feathers and fixed its beady eyes upon him, but it didn't fly away. Keita gave up and turned from the orchard, from his day's work, and walked down to the river that ran along his property.

He found a broad, smooth stone, and he sat there to contemplate the water. The river gurgled and flowed, and its melody soothed him, a balm for frayed nerves. He listened and watched and succumbed to the caresses of the spring breeze on his face. It was in such a beatific state that he first saw the bird.

She rose a few metres in front of him on blue-tinged wings. He admired the long beak, the crimson breast as bright as a wedding kimono. Her grace, the curve of her neck, made his heartbeat quicken. He had seen spindly legged egrets and mallards in this stream but never such a bird as this. In the deepest part of himself, he began to believe that this bird had been sent to him in this moment of difficulty to ease his pain. It was a wild idea, but he clung to it nevertheless.

He remained as still as the stone he sat upon, not wanting to spook this mysterious visitor. He watched as she dove into the water to catch a fish. The *ayu* wriggled in her beak, but she flew into a nearby tree and stunned the fish with a quick slap against the bark before gulping it down.

What kind of bird was she? And where had she come from? He would ask his friend Junji, a serious birdwatcher from way back. He had a life list of all the birds he wanted to see. Junji's vacations were always part of his quest to check off the birds on the list. He'd ventured as far away as Brazil to catch sight of a parrot in the wild. On a trip to the state of Washington, he'd been lucky enough to see a bald eagle. His mind was an encyclopaedia of bird lore.

Keita stayed by the river all morning watching the bird. He went back to the house for lunch, but he didn't tell Misa what he'd seen.

'How did your work go?' she asked him, dishing out curry over rice.

'Fine,' he said. He could not meet her eyes. He imagined Misa crying out in jealousy. 'What?' she might say. 'You prefer her company to mine? What about your family? Ichiro? Me?' But in reality, if he told her the truth she would have probably just chastised him for wasting the morning.

He returned to the riverside after lunch, but the bird was no longer there. After an hour's vigil, he went back to his pear trees. That night, he called Junji.

'Sounds like a kingfisher,' Junji said. 'But that's impossible. They don't live around here.'

'Maybe it got lost,' Keita said. 'Or it might have escaped from a zoo.'

'Or maybe you need new glasses.'

Keita didn't laugh. Tomorrow morning he would take his camera. He would show Junji that he wasn't dreaming.

The next day she was there, swooping through the trees on cobalt wings. He wondered if she had a nest nearby. He imagined eggs and then a flock of kingfishers flying through his mornings.

He hid in the bushes, and when the bird settled for a moment on a black pine branch, he clicked the shutter. He used an entire roll of film. At dusk he returned to the house, reluctantly.

'You're late,' Misa said over her shoulder. She was in the living room, seated on the straw-mat floor with the baby.

'I know. Sorry.' Keita saw his dinner laid out on the table and knew that it was already cold. He sat down to eat.

In the early days of their marriage, Misa would have sat down beside him while he dined, even if she had already eaten. But now the baby took up almost all of her time. Keita could hear her singing to him now: 'Flying crows, why do you call? 'Cause on the mountainside we've seven, seven little babies with lovely round eyes.'

She had the voice of a lark, but he hated that song. The crows that plagued his orchard were not pretty. They were like creatures from a nightmare. He'd heard of two schoolchildren being pecked by them. They dropped pebbles on the railroad tracks, messing up train schedules. So what if, according to legend, crows pulled the sun into the sky each day? The birds were a nuisance at best, and there was nothing lovely about their eyes.

He wanted to tell Misa to stop singing, but Ichiro began clapping his hands in delight.

The two of them were perfectly content without him. He felt like he was nothing more than a field hand or a houseboy.

When Keita developed the film a few days later, he was disappointed to find that none of the pictures had turned out. In some, the bird in flight appeared as a blur across the centre of the photo. Others were underexposed or awash with light. Nevertheless, he showed them to Junji.

'Could be a kingfisher,' Keita's friend mused, squinting at the glossy prints. 'But they're usually more skittish around humans.'

'I was well hidden,' Keita said. Or maybe he had a special affinity with the bird. Maybe she trusted him more than she did other people. This thought warmed him.

He considered telling Misa about the bird, waving the photos in front of Ichiro's face, but they had so much else to interest them—their songs, their kisses, their secret games. No, he would keep the bird for himself.

'Have you outwitted the crows?' Misa asked the next morning.

Keita sighed. He'd covered the trees with netting, but a few of the black demons had found an opening. Those that couldn't get in had spent the morning tormenting the cat.

'Crows are omnivorous,' Junji had told him. 'They'll eat anything.'

Even Kitty who slept at the foot of his futon? Well, maybe. He'd read an article in the newspaper about crows attacking baby squirrels in another town. The birds nudged the squirrels off the telephone wires and then ate them after they'd fallen to the ground. The reporter had called the birds 'a new type of serial killer'.

'Please don't speak to me about crows,' Keita told his wife. He knew that she didn't really care about what went on in the orchard. She was just making conversation. He wished they had more to talk about, like in the old days before their marriage when they had been a mystery to one another.

Keita knew that there was work to be done, but on this morning he didn't even pretend. He loaded his video camera with a fresh tape and marched straight to the riverbank. Why hadn't he thought of this earlier? With a video he would be able to capture the grace of the bird as well as her delicate shape and brilliant colours.

Keita crouched in his usual spot behind a bush. The grasses there had become matted from his daily vigils. He held his camera at the ready for an hour, and then two, but the bird—his bird—never showed. *The crows*, he thought, his stomach sickening. *The crows have murdered my lovely bird.* If they were brave enough to dive at humans and hungry enough to eat squirrels, then wouldn't they attack smaller birds as well? He tried to muster hope, but after five hours, he left the riverbank and returned to the house.

As usual, dinner was on the table, but Keita ignored the grilled fish and soup. He poured himself a cup of chilled sake and took a big gulp.

'What is it?' Misa asked, the baby on her lap. She had a rattle in one hand, and she reminded Keita of a court jester. There was no way she would ever be able to understand his sorrow.

In his dreams that night, the kingfisher glided on air, circling ever closer to Keita's hiding place. He sat transfixed. The bird, no bigger than a swallow, landed on his palm. She studied him with curious brown eyes and let him stroke her blue back with one finger. And then she ruffled her feathers and flew off into the sky.

Keita woke with a kernel of hope nestled in his heart. Today she would be there, waiting in the trees. He was sure of it as he bolted out the door without eating any breakfast. More than food, more than air, he needed a glimpse of his beautiful bird.

The sun rose higher in the sky as he stared at the river. The fish swam, undisturbed. Sparrows fluttered past, but there was no flash of blue. No long-beaked lover roosting on his palm. And then he heard a crack of twigs and saw the grasses twitch and part and there was Kitty, with a gift in her mouth. Keita stared in horror, not wanting to believe he had shared his bed with this animal.

The bird's once resplendent plumage was now matted and mauled. Its entrails leaked out through a ripped seam in its chest. One leg was bent, the claw dangling. Its bright eyes were now opaque, unseeing. A bright blue feather stuck to Kitty's fur like a macabre corsage. His eyes filled with tears. He took off his glasses, and the bird deposited at his feet by Kitty became as blurry as it appeared in the failed photos. The cat rubbed against his legs, and he kicked her away. For so long there had been nothing bright in his life, and then when this wonder appeared, he found joy. Yet he couldn't protect this wild thing from danger. And he couldn't protect his orchard—the trees that he had been entrusted with, that he was meant to maintain for Ichiro and all the generations to follow.

His hands trembled as he reached down and scooped up the dead kingfisher. The body was still warm, but there was no heart beating against his palm. With one thumb, he stroked the feathers, and then he laid the bird back down on the ground and began to dig with his bare hands. Dirt flew into the air. It fell on his head, but he didn't care. When he'd dug a deep-enough hole, he settled the carcass at the bottom and filled it back up. He found some large stones by the river and laid them on top of the grave. Then he crouched there, behind the bushes, and tried to rock the sudden loneliness out of his body. His grief was so absorbing that he didn't hear the bird calls at first.

'Kah! Kah!'

He looked over his shoulder and saw a black-headed figure flapping its wings. It was even larger than the jungle crows that harassed his orchard. The thing came closer and closer, but he wasn't afraid. Beside it, a taller creature picked through the grasses on elegant long legs, its pure white plumage dazzling in the sunlight.

He imagined being lifted by those great white wings, being carried away from the river, skimming over the tops of the pear trees in his orchard, and then continuing across the Pearl Bridge and beyond. He would leave all of this behind and travel to another country. Maybe he would work in an office, or in a clean, bright store. Maybe once he was gone, his wife and son would finally appreciate him. Perhaps they would think he had joined the ancestors and pray to his photo, setting out his favourite foods every morning at the altar. Meanwhile, in some other land, he would find respect and love. There would be no more crows, no more Kitty. He would begin again.

'We brought you breakfast,' a voice called out.

Keita stood up and shook away his fantasy. He brushed the dirt off his pants.

'You didn't eat,' the voice sang. 'You must be famished.'

His stomach rumbled as if in reply. He rubbed the tears from his eyes and put his glasses back on. Yes, he was hungry. Taking a deep breath, he flew to meet them, his wife and his child.

The Incan Ice Maiden

If she has enough grant money remaining after Asia, Solange will go to Peru. Just this morning, there was a picture in the *Japan Times* of Hillary Clinton observing an encased mummy shipped from Mount Ampato to Washington D.C. Juanita, they are calling her. She was beaten over the head and presented to the Incan gods. For the past five hundred years, she has been preserved in ice, like some kind of polar Sleeping Beauty who will never wake up.

Now, Solange is riding in a car down the narrow streets of Tokushima in Japan. Professor Tanaka, from the local university, is at the wheel. During their small talk earlier, he explained that Tokushima has the largest concentration of hospitals and coffee shops in the country and the fifth largest concentration of *yakuza* members. For the past few minutes, she hasn't been listening. She's been thinking about Juanita.

'This is the bridge I was telling you about,' he says as they approach a ramp. 'As you can see it is very old and narrow, but if we build a wider, more modern, bridge, the descendants might object.'

Solange nods, embarrassed that she hasn't been paying attention. She has waited for this chance for a very long time and she does not want to squander it in a muddle of jet lag. The grant couldn't have come at a better time. This project is just the thing she needs after the divorce and her failure, as a once-again single woman, to adopt a Bosnian war orphan. She has been drained not only psychologically, but also financially. Now, for the first time in a long time, she feels impassioned.

She has plans to write a book about human sacrifices. For the past two years, she has been lecturing anthropology students, showing them slides of faraway altars, when all along what she really wanted was to be in those places, to feel the spirits of long-lost maidens. She would like to travel to the top of that snowy volcano where Juanita, the 'Incan Ice Maiden', was found amidst pottery shards and llama bones.

Professor Tanaka takes her to a quaint little shop for *kaiseki ryori*. As they nibble tiny portions of the exquisitely prepared multi-course meal—a beancake presented on a perfectly formed maple leaf, fish eggs in a handcrafted pottery cup—Solange wonders if Professor Tanaka is flirting with her.

'Try holding your chopsticks like this,' he says, reaching across the table to touch her hand. She's been managing just fine, but he repositions her fingers higher on the lacquered cutlery. Solange feels a spark shoot from her fingers to her groin.

Professor Tanaka ('Call me Ken,' he says, after another drink) isn't her type. Solange has always gone for Slavic hunks. Nordic ski bums. Take Eric, for example. Her ex-husband was a perfect Aryan specimen with bleached blonde hair that made him look like an aging surfer, and bright blue eyes. All he lacked was height and width. Though pleasingly proportioned and still as fit as he'd been from collegiate lacrosse, Eric was only slightly taller than Solange.

Her taste in men has been developed through reading *GQ* in her teen years. Professor Tanaka—Ken—would have been too 'ethnic' for its glossy layouts. His longish hair gives him a bohemian look and his narrow chin is vulpine. At first glance, it would not have occurred to her to be attracted to him. Still, she is enjoying the slight pressure of his hand on hers and the way he seems to be peering into her soul.

His left ring finger is bare, but Solange knows that wedding bands are a Western custom, not entirely adopted in the East. Anyway, marriage often means something different here. The Japanese are not caught up in romantic fantasies of everlasting love like Americans, like Solange. She knows that marriages are still sometimes arranged here, that even young people consider lineage, income, and a potential bride's ability to serve tea properly before their nuptials.

She wonders if Professor Tanaka has children and, if so, what are their names? What do they look like? What kind of silly or precociously wise things do they blurt out at the dinner table?

When Solange sees a baby, even in a photograph, she feels a little ache in the region of her heart. Eric didn't want children—at least not within the next ten years and/or not with her. The child issue was one of the things wedged between them. Like an infection blossoming around a sliver of wood in skin, their troubles expanded from there.

That night, Solange beds down in her narrow hotel room and cocoons under starched sheets. Not even the neon flashing relentlessly through her window can keep her awake. She is exhausted.

At first, all is still and peaceful. Then she wakes within a dream. She pushes back a heavy blanket, breathes in the thin mountain air. In another part of the stone house, a woman is humming. Solange is no longer a thirty-five-year-old woman inclined to don Donna Karan power suits. She has somehow transformed into a young girl wrapped in a shawl.

The girl takes her time folding her bedding, running a comb through her hair. In the mirror she sees a budding beauty with blue-black hair and wide-open eyes, the colour of chocolate. She is too lovely for fieldwork. She will not be digging potatoes with her family. Her parents have another future in mind for her. Perhaps they will send her to school. She is imagining herself in a room with a teacher, filling her head with glorious things when the cry of a panicked alpaca fills the air. Shortly thereafter, a visitor announces himself in the courtyard.

Although the girl is mildly curious, she does not pay much attention to the words exchanged just outside the window. She idly notes that it is an important visitor. Her mother uses words of honour and respect.

The visitor's words, spoken gruffly, are unfamiliar: '. . . drought . . . volcano . . . sacrifice.' They mean nothing to her. But the news is not good because her mother begins pleading and crying. A chill sweeps through her body.

Solange wakes in a cold sweat.

'Some say the bridge is haunted,' Professor Tanaka tells her later at lunch. They are seated in a counter, dipping chopsticks into steaming bowls of noodles. The food is good and cheap and Solange is grateful for this introduction to ordinary fare.

'People believed that if a girl screamed or was afraid as she was thrown into the river, the spirits would not be appeased. The virgin had to be sacrificed willingly.'

Solange sips green tea from a handleless cup. 'It's hard to believe that anyone would ever go willingly.'

Professor Tanaka told her about the girls who were sent out to sea to quell storms or typhoons. Why always girls? Why not virgin boys?

In other cultures, men in the prime of life were served up to bloodthirsty gods. Solange thinks of the Mayans. Druids. The Celts sometimes stabbed men just to divine from their death throes, reading the future in the last twitching of muscles. Maybe, like Juanita, they were drugged with coca and alcohol before getting bashed in the head. In ancient Marseilles, the poor were persuaded to volunteer to be sacrificed. They were offered a year of fine dining in exchange for their lives. In the end, they were heaped with invectives. Then, drowned. Or stoned.

What is she doing here with her notebooks and pens and tape recorder? Why this affinity for altar-slain maidens? Why not study birthing rituals in tribal cultures? These are the questions that Solange has been asking herself. When Professor Tanaka asks, it's as if he's plucked the words from her brain.

'I think I was sacrificed in a previous life. It would explain my recurring nightmares. I have these dreams where the sky is spread above. My hands are bound. I cannot move. Drums throb all around me.' One look at Professor Tanaka's face tells her that she is being imprudent. Strange, at best. So she laughs and tries again.

'I've always been interested in human impulses. What is instinct? Is killing innate or learned behaviour?' She thinks of a man from her home town who was arrested for molesting a five-year-old girl. The police searched his house and found a shrine in his garage. The newspaper article was not specific, but it mentioned amulets and the blood of a goat.

On his stool beside her, Professor Tanaka nods slowly, thoughtfully. He raises his chopsticks to his mouth and his arm brushes against her breast.

Much of the city lies on reclaimed land. In Tokushima, there are bridges everywhere.

Every time Professor Tanaka's car creeps onto one of them, she thinks *Ophelia*. She thinks, *The bones of young women are everywhere.*

On one bridge she sees someone bent over the railing. It's an old woman with a hunched back and a sun-ripened face. She is peeling an orange, releasing the rinds to the wind and water below. Cars whiz past her heels, but she seems totally unaware. It's almost as if she were in another dimension. *Maybe she is a ghost*, Solange thinks. *Maybe she is feeding the virgins.*

Professor Tanaka drives by as if he hasn't even noticed. A few yards along the road, he swerves to avoid hitting an elderly man who is walking down the centre of the street. *They are like India's sacred cows*, Solange thinks. The old do not change their ways even in the face of progress. They wander about as if none of it exists.

Solange has been celibate for sixteen months, twelve days, and five hours. And counting. That last time was the bittersweet post-paper-signing, sayonara screw. She had bruises on her body for a week. It was like movie sex. When the bruises faded, first to brown, then yellow, then to skin, she had a good bawl. A week later, she found out that Eric was banging a twenty-year-old film student. She was making a documentary about convenience stores. 'A very intelligent young woman,' he told the friend of a friend. Big deal. Anyone can shoot a home movie with a video camera.

Now, in the cool of the museum, Solange cannot stop thinking about Professor Tanaka's hands. They are fine, almost feminine, and she is sure that they've never known the guts of a car, the gunk of a pipe. The fingernail of his pinky is long—signifying leisure class? Indolence? In ancient times, courtiers used their lengthened fingernails to scratch on the door of a lover—more refined than knocking. What would Professor Tanaka's nail feel like scraping down her bare back?

Later, after the museum, after dinner, there are fewer cars on the streets. Professor Tanaka drives wildly, recklessly, and this, too, excites her. On a sharp turn, she finds herself flung against the car door. 'Are you trying to kill us?' she asks. Her cheeks and neck are flushed.

'Oh, sorry,' he says. And slows down.

Solange feels oddly disappointed. This is her last night in Japan and she doesn't want it to end with a whimper. That bed is big enough for two. 'Would you join me for a drink?' she asks in front of her hotel.

There is just the slightest hesitation before he says 'yes'.

Months later, Solange is back in her Boston apartment. The notes, the photos, the taped interviews she has compiled are all strewn across the table. She picks up a folder and sighs. Where to begin? What would Margaret Mead do with all this information?

She wants to store it all inside her, keep it locked up like a secret. There is something indecent about flinging these lives into the public. She wants to throw a blanket over Juanita's body, roll her on a gurney to a quiet, private place.

For the moment, she pushes her papers aside. She has a distraction. Solange lays a palm on her belly and thinks, *How will I explain this to my parents?* A white baby—French-Canadian and German, with a splash of Scotch thrown in for good measure—would be forgivable. They would understand the leftover urges that might draw her and Eric together again, the new life that might then take root.

'In the eyes of the church you're still married,' her good Catholic mother would say. But almond eyes, toasty skin, a thatch of crow-black hair—these will cause confusion, hurt, possibly anger. Solange may be spending Christmas alone this year.

She always believed that a parent's love was unconditional and all-protective. For a long time, Solange imagined grief-stricken mothers tearing their hair and fathers attempting to bribe the oracles: 'I'll give you twenty pieces of gold if you pick that girl in the corner house instead.' But Solange knows that being chosen would probably have been an honour. The girls may have been excited about the dazzling afterlife that awaited them and the parents may have been puffed up and proud. Is that really so hard to conceive? Think of Jephthah who burned his beloved daughter. Think of Abraham who was willing to slice up his own son.

Solange decides to call her own mother. When she gets her on the phone she says, 'Mom, what would you have done if the voice of God had commanded you to sacrifice your only daughter?'

There is silence, and then a short laugh. 'I'd have gone to a head shrinker.'

'No, really, Mom.' Solange's mother once made a pilgrimage to the Vatican. She wears a silver cross between her breasts and eats fish on Fridays. 'What if you'd been absolutely sure it was God asking you to do this?'

'Did you have another one of those dreams, *cherie*?'

Solange is beginning to think that the idea of motherhood is fragile and arbitrary. Though she has stopped drinking wine and caffeinated beverages, she knows that this decision has nothing to do with instinct. There are parents in Southeast Asia who prostitute their daughters for televisions and refrigerators. Sometimes babies wash up on Brazilian beaches, victims of voodoo. For the first time, Solange is afraid of herself. How can she make sure that she will be a good parent? How will she keep her baby safe from harm?

And what to call this child, this wanted but accidental one, a stew of cultures in her womb? A name can be a curse or a talisman. In some Indian cultures children are not named until their personalities have emerged. In other societies, names change with the phases of a life.

Solange sometimes thinks of changing her own name. She is no longer Mrs Eric Lawrence and does not like to be linked even by a name to that man. (She has heard that he is currently in Baja with a nineteen-year-old violinist, the filmmaker having been traded in for new flesh.) Nor is she her sweet, unwed self, the girl who carried Indian arrowheads in pinafore pockets, the child who wanted to be a necromancer. What should she call herself now? Freewoman? Solange X?

At night Solange dreams she is lying on a slab of rock. She can feel its grainy, cold texture against her back. Her hands are tied behind her. Her ankles are lashed together tightly.

The rope burns into flesh. In the distance, llamas bleat warnings. The sky above is vast, blue, cloudless. A vulture slowly spirals and then glides away, biding its time.

She wants to close her eyes but she can't. She is damned to view it all—the bare-chested warrior who approaches at a measured pace, the sharpened stone in his fist, the circling vulture above.

Her heart pounds in time with the drumbeats. On her tongue is the tang of fear.

And then, suddenly, she becomes the warrior and she is no longer supine and awaiting slaughter but standing and free. The heavy knife is in her hand. The girl lying on the altar is not Solange. She is costumed in ceremonial finery—

striped blankets fastened with silver pins and a headdress fashioned of feathers. From underneath, her hair spills and shimmers like black liquid and her ochre eyes plead for mercy. They are surrounded by men with painted faces.

Solange runs to the girl and cuts the rope. The girl is so surprised that she can hardly move. Solange screams at her. 'Run, Juanita! Run!' And she saves her life.

In the morning, chickadees twitter at the window. New snow scintillates in the early light. The world seems, if only for a moment, a wonderfully benevolent place. A calm has spread throughout Solange's limbs and she realizes that she will never have those dreams again. Her bare feet meet the throw rug beside her brass bed and she takes her first steps of the day. Even now, she is moving towards her future, slashing through her fears to a wondrous new age.

She feels compelled to make an offering in gratitude. She envisions carefully arranged pyramids of hothouse fruit. Gold, frankincense, and myrrh. Or bricks of time stacked on an altar. She would trade her car and all of her electrical appliances for hard labour in order to celebrate this moment. But even as she considers all these possible gifts, she rubs her palm over her belly and knows that nothing will ever be enough.

Love After 9/11

'So what do you think of him?' Miranda asks, leaning across the table.

Candlelight is supposed to flatter women our age, but right now she looks ghoulish. The black spider-web shawl she's wearing falls off her shoulders, and she quickly hitches it back up.

I look away, in the direction of the men's room. 'I dunno,' I say. 'He's cute.'

We're only fifteen minutes into drinks, and this is my first time meeting Duncan, so really, what can I say? He's got a charming Virginian accent, old-world manners (holding the door open as we walked in, pulling out Miranda's chair when she sat down at the table), and a tight, fit body, from what I can tell. Also, Miranda has told me about the six-pack abs, and how many men over thirty have those?

I take a sip of my drink. 'Is he good in bed?' We are best friends, have been since we were roommates in college. I can ask that kind of thing.

She laughs a little nervously and glances over her shoulder. 'He's *amazing*.'

'Well, there you go.'

What I don't say is, 'How can you go out with a man who has killed people? How can you be sure that violence won't someday come out in his relationship with you?'

What I don't say is, 'My Japanese husband sometimes breaks the dishes when I serve him a meal made with tomatoes. The man I married pulls my hair when we are having sex (I can hardly call it making love any more) and won't stop even though I tell him it hurts. The mornings after, I find clumps of my hair on the pillow.'

Duncan comes back to the table. He sits down with a little bow, another one of those Southern mannerisms, just when the waitress appears with our food.

The menu is, of course, up to the minute. Whenever I visit New York City, Miranda brings me to the trendiest restaurants she can think of. A long time ago, we went to Balthazar, back when it was filled with models and actors, and another time we went to this place that I'd read about in *Elle* run by Picasso's grandson. Once, she took me to Windows on the World.

When we graduated from college, the plan was that I would go off to Japan for a year to have an adventure and to earn enough money from teaching English to pay off my student loans. I would come back and join Miranda in New York City. She wasn't all that interested in foreign travel; it was enough for her to visit her relatives in Mexico once in a while.

At any rate, we dreamed of hanging out in the Algonquin and going to parties with Jay McInerney.

I would write my novel about an all-girl punk rock band and Miranda would attend theatre productions off-off-Broadway and write reviews for the underground press. We'd date musicians and editors, with an occasional banker thrown in.

I wasn't especially into Japanese men. I remember walking through Central Park with Miranda, just before I left the country, saying, 'Don't worry. I've never been attracted to Asians. Well, maybe Ryuichi Sakamoto in *Merry Christmas, Mr. Lawrence*, but I think he might be gay.'

Of course, as it turned out, I liked Japan more than I'd expected—the food, the safety, the bowing gas station attendants—and then I met Kazu. Now I'm not sure if I could explain why I thought I could spend the rest of my life with him. I remember that he opened doors for me, making him seem ten times more polite than all of the other Japanese men I'd met. It's true that I was never bored when I was with him, and I believed our cultural differences would offer up endless interesting surprises. But really, we had nothing in common.

Miranda, who started crying when I called to tell her that I would be staying in Japan, maybe forever, thought our meeting was cosmic.

'If you've found the one, then you have to stay,' she told me. 'But I'll really, really miss you.'

The one. That's how we talked back then, how Miranda still talks sometimes.

It's true that I felt nauseated and short of breath whenever I thought about leaving Kazu. I thought I might shrivel up and die a bitter spinster if I did not marry him. But who's to say I wouldn't have felt differently after a year back in the States?

All evening I watch the two of them, how they lean into each other, how, already, they are finishing each other's sentences and stories. Every once in a while, Duncan brings Miranda's hand to his lips and each kiss seems like a sacrament.

When she goes to the bathroom, Duncan leans forward as if he's about to tell me a secret. 'Miranda says you're a writer. I scribbled some poems while I was over there in the desert. I'm wondering if you'd be willing to take a look.'

A warrior and a poet!

I bite my lips, trying to come up with an excuse to say no.

'I wrote some poems for Miranda too.' Here, he blushes. 'I was thinking I'd read them at the ceremony.'

The ceremony? I study his hands, now flat on the table. I imagine those fingers gripping a pen as he gazes at acres of glittering sand. I imagine them drifting over Miranda's skin like water gliders.

'Sure,' I say. 'Why don't you send them to me by e-mail?' And then, because I can't help myself, I add, 'We've been friends for half our lives. That's a long time.' *Far, far longer than you've known her.* 'Be nice to her.'

He looks a bit puzzled. 'I would cut out my heart for her.'

I keep my eye on him all evening, till he packs us into a cab and sends us home, to Miranda's apartment.

She is all giggly. I can't tell if it's because of all the drinks or because she's fallen in love.

'So how serious is it?' I ask her.

'He asked me to marry him.'

'Really. That serious, huh?' I can't believe I had to ask. Once, she would have called me, breathless, after every single date. At one time, I would have told her how, sometimes I wake up at night and see Kazu sitting in front of the computer with his cock in his hand. I checked one morning and found that he had bookmarked HotAsianBabes.com.

'So what did you say?' I ask Miranda.

'I told him I would think about it,' she says. 'I love him, I really do, but I've got so much baggage. I feel like damaged goods.'

This is so typical of her. I roll my eyes.

Then she says, 'I'm worried that he'll get hurt. He's never been married before. He said he's never felt this way about anyone, but I've been there. I don't want to be the agent of his disillusionment.'

Seriously. She actually said, 'agent of disillusionment'.

I laugh without meaning to. 'He's a sniper. I bet he can take care of himself.'

When she turns to me, her eyes are so cold that I think I may have lost her forever.

'Sorry,' I say quickly. 'It's just, well . . . don't you ever think about that part of him?'

'He's out of the military now, Sofie,' she says slowly, as if she's explaining to a child. 'He's not even in favour of this war.'

'But don't you think that being over there had some effect on him?'

She shrugs and then I know that she sees him as another one of her broken-winged birds, someone she can take care of. It doesn't bode well.

There was another reason I went to Japan. Besides the adventure and the student loan, I mean. I was fleeing heartbreak. I had this belief that if I could get far enough from the pain, it would just go away.

Miranda didn't really think that much of Eddie to begin with. She thought that he talked too much, and didn't take my art seriously enough. That he simply didn't understand. For example, he had been unimpressed by my personal rejection from *The Paris Review*, whereas Miranda had sprung for champagne. 'I mean, c'mon. *The Paris Review!* He doesn't even know what it is,' Miranda had crowed. 'He's a philistine!'

She also thought I deserved someone better looking, but I would have run into a burning building for him. I would have borne seven children for that guy. That's how I felt back then, before he broke my heart.

'He's nothing,' Miranda told me as she sat there with the box of tissues. She plucked one out and handed it to me. 'Some day you will meet someone so much better.'

By the time Eddie wrote to me saying that he was sorry and that he wanted us to be back in touch, I was engaged. I had the rock on my finger. We'd reserved the hall. My parents had confirmed their plane reservations—Columbia, South Carolina, to Detroit to Osaka. I wrote back to Eddie and told him about the wedding. Part of me wanted him to call up asking for a second chance, just to see what I would do. But he didn't, and I married Kazu, as planned.

Miranda got married a couple of years later, to someone we both knew from college. I wanted her to be happy, of course, but I didn't really expect it to last. He cheated on her over and over, and she finally got tired of forgiving him.

Early on, I told Kazu that if he was ever unfaithful to me or if he hit me, I would leave him. After all, I was giving up a lot for him—the Algonquin, good radio stations, Jay McInerney. My country.

He didn't look at other women, but we fought almost from the beginning. We disagreed, loudly, about the décor. He wanted the faux cachet of Monet water lily prints while I wanted bright abstracts by my art major friends on the walls. On vacation, he wanted to go to Guam while I wanted to visit my family. And then, later, we'd argue about whether or not women forced into prostitution during WWII should be compensated or whether, as an American, I should express remorse to our elderly neighbour, who was from Nagasaki, or whether the United States should have military bases in Okinawa.

It was never boring, but it was never easy either.

He would sometimes call me away from something that I was deeply engaged in—a short story I was writing, a book I was reading—if a famous American appeared on TV. Sometimes I would watch, just to be polite, as Cyndi Lauper, or whoever, endured silly interview questions on some Japanese variety show. Other times, I would become irritated. 'I don't want to watch TV right now,' I'd say. 'I was busy doing something!'

One evening, after being beckoned, I sat down next to him to watch a segment about the filming of *The Lord of the Rings*. It was interesting enough, but I hated being summoned like that, from some far corner of the house. I sighed loudly, and he cuffed me on the head. I spent the whole night wondering if I should leave him. I'd promised, after all.

Months later, I was checking my e-mail on the computer in the bedroom. Kazu was watching TV in the living room, as usual.

'Sofie,' he called out. 'Hurry up! Come look at this!'

I sighed. Probably Michael Jordan promoting new shoes. I dragged myself away from the computer and stalked down the hallway, entering the living room just in time to see the second tower get hit.

Back at Miranda's apartment, we kick off our shoes and sink into the sofa. For the first time this evening, she takes off the shawl. It's then that I see the bruise on her upper arm. Five fingers. A man's hand.

'What the hell is this?' I ask her.

She glances over. 'Oh, that.'

I wait.

'I was about to step into traffic and he grabbed me. To save me.'

The way she tells it, I find myself wanting to believe her.

'Do you want some water?' she asks, getting up off the sofa. 'I could really use a tall, cold glass of water.'

Kazu would deny this later, but when the towers started to fall, he laughed a short bitter laugh and said, 'Remember Hiroshima.'

I thought then that anyone who hated the United States as much as he did could not possibly love me, an American.

In the days following, the 12th, the 13th, the 14th, neighbours and colleagues at the school where I taught

English kindly offered their sympathies. They inquired if I had lost anyone in the tragedy, and when I said no, they nodded and never spoke of it again.

'You should be here with us,' Miranda said when I called her on the phone. 'I hate that you're over there, all alone.'

But I didn't want to be there. I remembered going back to the States during the first Gulf war, and walking into K-Mart. All those Desert Storm coffee mugs and T-shirts! All those yellow ribbons! I wanted my distance. I had perspective.

The Japanese surrounding me quickly lost interest. They were still dealing with the sarin in the Tokyo subway. Hell, some of them, like my husband, who was born in 1963, were still dealing with the atomic bomb.

When the United States started tearing up the desert, Kazu shook his head and muttered, '*Yappari*,' which translates as something like 'Just what I expected from those American goons.'

Miranda said, 'I read that the soldiers are writing the names of the victims on the bombs before dropping them. Maybe I shouldn't say this, but it makes me feel good.'

On the last day of my visit, Miranda takes me down to Ground Zero.

In the long nights after, Miranda came down here to serve coffee to the firefighters who were digging through the debris. She told me how, at the time, only a week before 9/11, she'd been hit on in an Irish bar by some fireman. 'He was sweet,' she said, 'But I couldn't see myself living the life of a firefighter's wife, worrying every time he went out on a call.' Here, she chokes up. 'But now I feel so bad about blowing him off. I could have gone out with him just once. I could have given him a chance.'

Today, I look up at the empty sky where the towers used to be and say, 'Eddie Ryan was one of the victims.'

Miranda's mouth falls open. 'What? You never told me.'

I drop my eyes and scuff the dirt with my shoe. 'Well, it wasn't *the* Eddie Ryan. It was a guy with the same name. "A great father and husband." CEO of his company, but he still showed up for all of his son's Little League games.' Miranda nods solemnly.

'I made sort of a shrine for him,' I say. 'I lit a candle for him every night for six months.'

In the winter, I planted tulip bulbs—one for Edward, one for his wife and each of his children, and all of the children that I knew by then I would never have. When they came up in the spring, I vowed to repair my broken marriage. I'd do it all by myself.

Miranda reaches over and squeezes my hand.

A couple of weeks later, I'm sitting in the departure lounge in Detroit, waiting for the plane that will take me back to Japan. I've got a sack of sandwiches packed by my mother, a paperback, my notebook, some pens.

I rifle through my stuff, then look up to see a group of Army recruits coming towards the gate. Their uniforms are pressed and clean, their faces fresh, unwrinkled. Their innocence makes me want to weep. For a moment, I think of running over to them and telling them, 'Do. Not. Get. On. That. Plane.' I imagine grabbing them, hard enough to leave an imprint, and peering into their untroubled eyes.

They'll be different when they get back. Broken, maybe. Haunted. They will need someone to care for them as never before.

My mind flashes to Miranda and Duncan at that restaurant table, the tender way they handled each other. The hurt that they both harbour inside.

I take out my cell phone and punch out her number.

'Hello?'

'Miranda, I'm calling to give you my blessings,' I say.

After all, what the hell do I know about love?

Down the Mountain

You say that you want to leave this mountain, daughter, and I know that your will is strong. For you, there is not enough of life in selling fish-on-a-stick or serving noodles to strangers. You look at the swaying vine bridge and see a magnet for tourists, those busloads of people who come up from the city, filling the valley with sounds of laughter and loud voices. I will not stand in your way, but before you go, there are some things that you must know.

I will tell you our story once again. You've heard parts of it before, I know, when you were a child, too little to be able to tell the difference between fairy tales and family lore, and again when you were a teenager, stubborn and deaf to a mother's wisdom. Now I think you are ready to understand the meaning of that bridge and the things that brought us here.

Long, long ago, my daughter, our people lived far from these trees, this valley, that gurgling brook. They inhabited a grand palace in the ancient capital of Kyoto. Our women—oh, our women—wore the finest silk kimonos woven by master craftsmen. As they roamed the palace halls, the silk whispered on the hardwood floors behind them. Their days were filled with infinite pleasures—the plucked strings of a koto, the beauty of a newly blossomed camellia, the anticipation of a lover's poem. There were no dishes to wash, no futons to beat in the sun, no floors to sweep. Our women were ladies of leisure who passed their time playing games with painted sea shells and composing *waka*. Their lives were so beautiful that it pains my heart to think of it now. But this gilded existence came to an end.

A war began between the armies of our people and the soldiers of the Shining Prince. The enemy warriors rode in on their horses, torching temples and thatched roofs, terrorizing our women and children.

The emperor's mother declared that she would let no one usurp her small son. She gathered her boy and his precious relics—a mirror, a sword, and a lacquer box—and fled the capital. They dove into the sea—death, their only hope of escape—and the relics sank to the sandy bottom to become the wonder of fish and octopus and all the other creatures of the deep.

Our people had no ruler, no father to guide and protect them. They were forced to flee the once glorious capital. Under cover of night, they set off for the wilds of Shikoku, this island to the west. Here, high in the mountains, they found their hiding place on the edge of a wide ravine.

They wove vines into ropes and created a bridge on which they could cross the ravine. On the other side, there were berries to be picked, wild mushrooms, and rambling boar. Everything they needed was on these mountains and for decades and then centuries, they lived their lives in seclusion, afraid of what was down below.

Do you remember, my daughter, the first time I took you across that bridge? You rode on my back and you were not afraid. Even as a child of three, your courage was something to behold. And you knew exactly what you wanted.

'Give me a baby sister,' you pleaded, tugging at my leg. As if a little girl could be bought like a bag of rice. You'd seen the swaddled sibling of your friend Mariko and you'd thought that a mewling babe was just another toy.

Then you looked up and saw the tears filming my eyes and said, 'What's wrong, Mama? Do you want a baby sister too?'

What I could not tell you then, I will tell you now. I was crying not out of grief, but out of gratitude. The day of your birth—a day of bird song and plum blossoms—was the happiest day of my life. I remember lying against the buckwheat pillows, overcome by exhaustion but still awake enough to count your fingers and toes, to look into your newborn eyes and see that you were alert to the world. Each day as I watched you grow, I thanked the ancestors and the gods of the mountains and valleys that you were such a bright and happy child.

I could not tell you then that I longed for a sister too. But my sister was not a wish-born phantom. She was a brown-skinned beauty with scabbed knees and the voice of a nightingale, a flesh-and-blood playmate with tangled hair. My sister. I never told you about Mitsuko. How we slept cuddled together during the long nights of winter. How we folded paper dolls side by side. How we ran shrieking through the forest, pretending to escape the Shining Prince of our elders' stories.

Mitsuko was a year older than me and twice as beautiful. She had the long, thin face and almond-shaped eyes of the courtiers of old. Her hair was long and black like mine, but thicker and stronger. If woven, her hair would have made a fine rope for swinging over the gorge.

We played through our days as girls do, acting out all of the stories that we'd heard. She was the Lady of Gion; I, her lady in waiting. She was the favoured dancing girl of Lord Kiyomori, and I was the one who combed her hair. She was the moon princess sent to earth as punishment; I, the suitors at her door.

'I am the moon princess,' she said, seated on a carpet of leaves.

'Please,' I said, 'Will you marry me?'

'Only if you bring me a jewelled branch from paradise.'

I went off into the woods and, because there were many suitors in the story, returned with a different voice. 'Oh moon princess, won't you marry me? I have a grand house—the finest in Kyoto.'

'I will marry you if you bring me the begging bowl of Buddha.'

And so, we continued in our play.

Until one autumn night, when the full moon glowed beyond the flaming leaves, my sister went into the yard alone and began to cry.

'Take me back to you,' she wailed into the heavens. 'I am the moon princess and I want to go home.'

I heard her voice, heard her sing her plea. I ran out into the yard to join her, pine needles sticking to my bare feet. 'Me, too,' I shouted. 'Fly me to the moon!'

But my sister did not turn and welcome me into her game. She reached up into the air and began to keen. The sound that she made was not human. It was the voice of an animal caught in a trap. My skin prickled with fear. And then my parents ran out of the house.

I remember my mother's face, the 'O' of her mouth, the fingers raking her cheeks in despair. Her *nemaki* came loose with her sudden movement as she rushed to my sister's side.

My father slid his rough palm over my head, down to cover my eyes. And though I could not see Mitsuko, I heard her thrashing and kicking on the pine-needled ground.

My mother and father explained to me later that Mitsuko was stricken by an illness that would never be cured. It had been in her blood from long ago. They told me that the illness was a secret and I had to promise not to tell.

When I was old enough, I left our thatched-roof house in the mornings for the one-room school. I crossed the vine bridge, careful not to look down, down, down, holding tight to its twine rail, then skipped along the solid mountain path.

I made new friends at the school. They were children from other villages nestled among the trees. They had brothers and sisters and we all played together. I did not tell them about Mitsuko.

My sister stayed in the house with my granny and my mother. She played out her stories alone. Sometimes she rocked in the corner, singing a song: 'Though the wind doth not blow, the vine bridge sways to and fro.'

One day when my mother was off gathering wild mushrooms and my granny was ailing abed, Mitsuko escaped from the house and into the forest.

My mother found her, but not before a hunter's eyes had fallen upon her gentle curves. Not before a great desire had swept the hunter's sense away.

That night, as my family slept around the brazier, quilts piled high upon us, I heard the door slide open. I lay still in my nest of feathers and flannel and watched a shadowy man enter the room. He must have held his breath because he did not make a sound. I could not even hear his white-socked feet gliding on our bare wooden floors.

I was not sure if I was dreaming or not. I waited for some sign. Then the man bent over my sister who slept against the wall. I saw her rise from under the covers and follow this stranger into the moonlight. And I did not say a word. Perhaps I should have, but when morning came, Mitsuko was in her bed once again.

A month later, in the clear light of day, a hunter came to our door with a freshly-killed boar.

'I offer this for your daughter,' he said, laying the carcass at my father's feet.

A man offering a dowry? This behaviour was most bizarre.

'You are asking for Hideko?'

The hunter shook his head. 'No, I have come for your first daughter. The one you call Mitsuko.'

My father stepped away from the boar as if it were bad luck. 'Impossible. She will stay in this house until the day she dies.'

The hunter fell to his knees. He was young, his face yet unbearded. A fever had tinged his cheeks. Through a crack in the wall, I saw the sickness of the heart for the first time.

The hunter bowed his head. 'My love for your daughter is as deep as that ravine.'

'Impossible,' my father repeated. 'That girl is mad.'

My parents began to bar the doors and windows at night. A few weeks later, when Mitsuko's blood refused to flow, they took her down the mountain to a place where I'd never been.

I did not go with them, but I heard afterwards how Mitsuko bit the man in the white coat. How she flew at the windows and smashed them with her fists. How she didn't stop fighting until a nurse pressed a handkerchief to her face. It was not until I was much older—almost as old as you—that I understood what they had done to her.

When Mitsuko came back up the mountain, she left her spirit behind.

I sat in the corner with her and whispered as in the days of old. 'Let's fly to the moon,' I said. 'That's where we belong.'

She said nothing in return. Her smile was blank and devoid of memory. She reached for a strand of my hair and then she put it in her mouth.

'Now, now,' I said. I patted her like a baby. Like all the babies she would never have.

I was away at school the next time she escaped. I knew nothing of the turmoil that surrounded the house on that day. I sat in a classroom with twelve other children painting kanji on thin, white paper. Meanwhile, my father gave up on roof-thatching to search through the forest with my mother, but they did not find Mitsuko.

The stars were beginning to flicker when I reached the vine bridge on my way home. The moon was already full and bright. I took my first step over the gorge and then I saw my sister on the other side. She was completely naked. She must have been hiding, waiting for my return. I could hear her singing, 'Take me home, take me home.'

'Mitsuko!' I shouted.

For a moment, I believed that we were small girls again, about to begin another happy adventure beneath the boughs of pine trees. But in the middle of the bridge, my sister stopped and crawled up over the railing.

I must have cried out, but I don't remember. All I see, even now, is her body flying through the air, her arms spread like wings, her long black hair streaming behind her. I heard her singing all the way down and I cursed the moon for listening.

My daughter, I have never been to the cities below this mountain. I do not understand the people who live there—them with their knives and lies and slovenly ways. The world of our ancestors is long past, the painted shells shattered and swept away.

Those below, they will not understand why a wonderful girl like you gazes at the night sky. They will not allow you to speak to the spirits that guide you. Our mountain ways are queer to them. But leave, if you must.

I have told you the secrets of our family so that they will not be forgotten and so that my sister's spirit will live in your heart. The past is etched in your skin. It flows in your blood and no one can erase it.

River of Dolls

Junko hauled a big carton out of the closet. Every February she did this—pulled the box out of the closet where the spare futons were stored, opened the cardboard flaps, and began taking out the dolls, the multi-level stand, the red cloth, the miniature plum trees, and tea set. For years she had prepared the display alone, in silence, knowing that neither would there be a little girl to admire the crowned empress doll in her layers of brocade kimono nor the finely crafted instruments of the more lowly musicians.

As a child, Junko had watched her mother set up this very same display. She kneeled on a cushion at the base of the stand as her mother arranged the dolls one by one—the emperor at the top; then the imperial guards in their suits of armour; the ladies-in-waiting, who brushed the empress' long hair and wrote poetry on gilded fans; down to the court jesters and the bearers who transported the royal couple in a palanquin hefted onto their shoulders. When the last courtier was in place, when the archer was positioned with his bows and arrows, and the tiny lacquer mirror had been prepared for the empress, Junko's mother turned to her with her favourite doll.

'Here, I'll let you put this one on top,' she said.

Usually, Junko would not have been allowed to touch the fragile and expensive dolls. But her mother trusted her for as long as it took to lift the empress with two hands and set it next to the emperor. Then she would sink back into the cushion and dream herself into the dolls' world.

When she grew up, she would marry a prince. It was possible. Look at Empress Michiko. One day she was a commoner playing tennis at a resort in Karuizawa, then, not long after, a bewigged bride in twelve layers of kimono. Michiko-sama's story was like a fairy tale and little Junko believed that if an ordinary girl could marry a descendant of the sun goddess, then perhaps an old childless couple really could split a peach and find a baby boy inside. Maybe there really was a rabbit making rice cakes on the moon.

In her childhood, Junko had never wondered why all of the dolls were adults. 'Where are your children? The princes and princesses?' she asked now.

The white-faced couple stared back at her.

She leaned in to study the painted eyebrows of the empress. 'Or can't you produce an heir?'

Back in the Heian Period, men were allowed concubines. Barren empresses had to make way for their husbands' mistresses. 'And what if he is the cause?' Junko asked the doll. She nodded to the emperor who sat with his hands folded around a fan. Well, never mind. She couldn't blame him. 'It must be stuffy in that box,' she said to change the subject. 'I'm sorry for keeping you cooped up in the dark.'

When she was small, Junko and her neighbourhood playmates gathered in front of the display on 3 March, the day of the Girl's Festival, and snacked on pastel-coloured rice balls. Her best friend, Emi, lived in an apartment too small to accommodate such a grand collection. She had a tinier set made of plaster, which could not compare to Junko's seven red-carpeted tiers.

The very next day, Junko watched as her mother carefully packed the dolls away, wrapping each in cocoons of tissue before committing them to their yearly confinement.

'If we wait too long, you won't be able to get married,' Junko's mother said. 'It's bad luck to leave the dolls up.'

Junko had vowed to remember this.

Now, all these years later, unfolding the tiny gold screen, she thought that her mother must have stowed them away on time. After all, Junko was an adult and she was not a spinster. She'd married Yuji five years ago.

Junko had gone through her twenties without any prospects. In high school, there was a boy—a quiet, awkward boy who excelled at the game of *igo*. They kissed, once, behind a convenience store, their mouths tasting of lemon soda. Nothing had ever come of it. Still living under her parents' roof at the age of thirty, Junko realized that her life would never be like a fairy tale. And so when her father offered to have her introduced to a fortyish-year-old chemist whose wife had died, she was resigned yet grateful.

They met for the first time in the lobby of the Tokyu Inn. Junko arrived a minute late, wearing a dark grey suit and her hair pulled back into a knot. She pushed through the revolving doors and the slow click of her heels on marble echoed throughout the cavernous hall. There was no one waiting for her, only scattered clusters of young women sipping coffee, plumped shopping bags at their feet. For a moment she wondered if he had changed his mind. Perhaps he'd detected something in her photo that he did not like—her close-set eyes, her melted chin. Or he might have found someone else.

Junko drifted away from the brightly clothed women and their chatter to the glass-fronted case near the entrance. 'For Your Happy Wedding' a banner read in English. And there was a dress. A bridal gown, one of several that could be rented for a hotel wedding. Junko longed for the ivory silk, the bugle beads, the long flowing train. Would she ever get to wear such a beautiful dress?

Yuji's photo was in her purse. She had brought it along just in case, although she'd already memorized his image. She knew his broad face and his hunger-hollowed cheeks. His black hair was unfashionably parted at the side and he hadn't dyed the white strands at his temples, but she was moved by these signs of neglect. He was in need of care.

In the photo he did not smile, but the crinkles at the corners of his eyes suggested a certain kindness. And the creases engraved in his forehead were like scars of worry. She could already see that he was a tender man.

The door spun behind her then and she turned from the white lace to see him. He stood still, his eyes searching, and Junko noted that he was shorter than she'd imagined. He was wearing a navy suit and a striped tie.

She approached him. '*Hama-san*?'

His head snapped in her direction and when he saw her, his face eased into a smile. 'Miss Tanaka?'

She already knew about the young wife who had died, the house on the river, and his annual salary. He worked at a pharmaceutical company and his hobby was golf. When they sat down in the velvet-upholstered chairs in the centre of the lobby, they ordered tea and spoke of flowers.

'I have a rose bush in my garden,' Yuji said, 'but it didn't bloom this year.'

'I have tended roses before,' Junko said, lowering her eyes. 'Perhaps I could help you.'

Now, on this February morning, Junko gazed out the window at the river that flowed by, just past the edge of their property. She remembered how happy she had felt on the day of her engagement. How hopeful. She pressed her hands to her abdomen and allowed herself a smile.

Yuji did not like the dolls, arranged in hierarchical order. 'Our country is a democracy now,' he'd said. 'Those hina dolls, like Kimi-ga-yo, are just another reminder of the empire that got us into trouble.' He did not sing that anthem to the emperor during ceremonies. He even objected to the way Junko had first prepared his lunch—with the red pickled plum centred in the square of white rice in imitation of the flag.

'No one thinks that way about the dolls,' she usually chided. 'They're pretty, that's all.'

Turning her attention once again to the display, she arranged the paper lanterns, and the tiny vases in which she inserted bouquets of flowers. She thought of her wedding.

The ceremony was held only two months after their first meeting, in another hotel across town. Junko's boss gave a ten-minute speech, praising her efficiency and gentle ways. Her co-workers sent an envelope of money.

After the honeymoon in Okinawa, she returned to the office where she had worked for almost ten years. As she was passing out souvenirs from the trip—black sugar candies—the others teased her.

'That's it. You'll quit now and go off to have babies,' one man said.

A younger woman, a recent college graduate, regarded her with envy. 'I wish I could get married and stay home. I'm tired of working.'

And Akira, who had never looked at her as a woman before, winked and said, 'Looks like marriage agrees with you.'

Junko blushed, remembering the stains on white sheets and Yuji's moans.

In the following days, she sometimes found herself staring at her wedding band, lost in daydreams of domestic bliss. Someday she would have a baby and resign, but for now, Yuji had encouraged her to keep working. 'You might get bored around the house,' he said. 'I want you to be happy.'

Yuji considered himself a modern man. He had been to the United States, shaken hands with female researchers, and taken notes from their lectures. His mother had taught high school throughout his childhood. He believed that women wanted careers.

For Junko, however, the appeal of office life had long since evaporated. She was tired of the navy uniform that she wore day after day, sick of the sound of ringing phones. She preferred the scent of freshly laundered clothes to that of the smoky office.

She was happiest at home, in her new domain. There, she could step into sunlight with her straw hat and trowel and dig into the soft, fresh earth. Little by little, she transformed the weedy patch into a spot of paradise. The lilies and roses responded to her care at once. Every season brought new blossoms—the camellias of winter, irises and daffodils in the spring, then roses, hydrangeas, morning glories, and marigolds in autumn.

But nothing grew in her womb.

Yuji did not speak of children, nor of their fumblings in the dark. Most of his contemporaries worked long hours and had little time for their families. Their children had grown into bewildering strangers no longer in need of a father's protection. Yuji probably thought that children were solely a woman's concern. It was possible that he had never held a baby.

She had wondered about his first wife. Once, when she had asked him about their desires for children, he had looked at her across the table in surprise. She knew from his stricken expression that the grief was always within him, lurking beneath the surface. It rose to his skin with one question. She wished she could take it back.

'Yes, we wanted children,' he said, 'but she became ill soon after our marriage. After that, all I wanted was for her to survive.'

Once again Junko felt as if she were fading and she remembered that another woman had lived in those rooms.

Yuji seemed to sense her sudden loneliness. He smiled sadly. 'Let us not think of the past, Junko. We have a new life together.'

Junko waited. Months and then a year passed, but her belly didn't grow. She counted days on the calendar. She ate sweet potatoes. She made offerings at the temple of the dog, the spiritual protector of pregnant women, but nothing happened.

'I've been to the hospital,' she finally told Yuji. They were watching TV. 'There's nothing wrong with my body.'

Yuji's gaze shifted from the baseball game to her face. 'What did you say?'

'There's no reason why I can't have a baby. It must be—well, would you go in for a test?'

A cheer rose in the room as the Hanshin Tigers scored another run, but Yuji did not react.

Later, at the hospital, the elderly doctor explained why Yuji would never be able to father a child. He delivered the news in the fluorescence of his office. Yuji sat still as if he hadn't heard, but Junko's eyes flitted wildly around the room. The framed diploma, the poster of a skinless man, the doctor's white coat—wasn't there something that could help them?

'Isn't there a cure?' Junko asked.

The white-haired doctor took off his glasses and pinched the bridge of his nose. 'I'm sorry,' he said. 'I know that this is a difficult thing.' He left them alone then to absorb the shock in private.

They inquired about adopting a baby, but there were so many other couples who wanted a child just as badly—couples with more money and better connections. Yuji began to speak of getting a dog.

'Or we can travel,' he said. 'We haven't done much of that, have we? We could go to Bali or Australia. There's really nothing holding us back.'

But Junko didn't think that she would be able to bear the sight of other people's children, the well-intentioned questions of brand-new tour group acquaintances. She didn't want to look at the toddler-sized T-shirts in the gift shops, the children's meals on menus, preferring the quiet interior of her house and the privacy of her walled garden.

Now, Junko placed the palanquin and a horse-led cart on the bottom tier of the stand and stepped back to admire her work. The dolls seemed to be watching her.

When she was small, her mother had taken her to a special temple in distant Wakayama. There, the priests gathered unwanted dolls and burned them in an annual ceremony. In ancient Japan, people believed that dolls had souls. Women rubbed their sins and sorrows into the skin of the dolls and tossed them out to sea, where the cleansing waters would purify them. Nowadays, there were few who held these beliefs, but many girls who'd outgrown their dolls and needed to make room for their electronic organs and tennis rackets and computer games. And so the dolls, some of them still beautiful and hardly worn, were brought by the basketful to the temple. When Junko, a tiny girl, had seen the piles of unwanted dolls, she had been filled with sadness. 'They are not alive,' her mother told her. But in that temple Junko had felt their souls swirling around her.

The sound of voices came to her from outside, tugging her from memory. Children were on their way home from school and their laughter rang out in the late afternoon. Junko could hear the splash of water as little boys heaved rocks into the river. She pressed a palm to her stomach. In another country there might have been a better solution. She'd read of artificial insemination and in vitro fertilization. But here, considering their limited means, she and Yuji were subject to fate. They had almost no way to counter their bad luck.

Two of Junko's co-workers had married in the years since her wedding. Both had become pregnant within six months. At work, Junko sometimes stumbled into chats about weird cravings and names and nurseries, but when the others became aware of her presence, they lowered their voices and drifted apart. Why was it so easy for them? She thought of Akira whose wife had given him twins.

She had brought Akira tea every morning. She ran errands for him and typed documents at his request. He told her that he was married to his high school sweetheart and now had three children, but this didn't stop him from flirting with every woman who stepped into the office.

'Mami-chan, what are you doing after work?' he asked the insurance woman who came around once a week. 'I'm single tonight.' The other men in the office laughed at his bravado. They probably envied his ease with women, his thick glossy hair and wide eyes that made people think of foreign actors. But Junko always lowered her eyes when he made such a remark. Now, she no longer worked with

Akira, and she didn't want to think of him. She'd quit her job two weeks before.

Yuji would be coming home soon. He worked very hard for them—for her—sometimes leaving the house before sunrise. Junko's job was to make the home a haven, a place where Yuji could forget all the cares of the day. She made sure that there were fresh flowers in the alcove, that the futons were aired every morning, and that all of Yuji's shirts were pressed and starched. Some evenings she gave him back rubs or massaged his feet.

Junko set to work chopping carrots and daikon, soaking dried seaweed for the miso soup, salting the red snapper she'd bought earlier in the day from the corner fish monger. By the time Yuji slid open the door, the house was infused with dinner smells.

'*Tadaima!*' he called out.

'*O-kaeri*,' Junko said, welcoming him.

When they'd first been married, their relationship had been characterized by polite attentiveness. Neither one of them had known exactly how to behave. By now, Yuji's habits were familiar to her. Without looking she knew that he was stepping out of his shoes and aligning them in the entryway. Next, he would slide his feet into slippers and make his way to the bedroom where he would remove his jacket and tie. She heard the jingle of dropped keys, the flush of the toilet, the scuff of slippers on wood. And then he was in the kitchen with his shirt partly unbuttoned, his T-shirt visible underneath.

'I see you set up the dolls,' he said.

Junko nodded, eyes downcast.

She kept her silence, letting the moment pass.

Yuji crept up behind her. 'Here, let me help you with something.' He reached for the rice cooker.

Usually, the little dishes of pickled radishes and rice and fish were set on the table by the time Yuji walked in the door. On this evening, however, Junko had made egg custard and her timing was off. 'Sit down,' she said. She shooed him towards the head of the table. 'It's almost ready.'

He lingered a few breaths longer, then sat in his chair.

Junko dished out the hot sticky rice and placed a bowl of it before him. Then the fish, the soup, the custard. 'Eat, eat,' she said. 'Before it gets cold.' She watched him as he picked up his chopsticks and pinched a morsel of fish.

'I haven't had *tai* since the New Year holidays,' he said.

Junko turned to the stove. She thought of telling him then that they had something to celebrate, but the words seemed to float apart in her mind. And so she said, 'Today red snapper was on sale, that's all.'

They ate together in silence. Few words ever passed between them, but Junko felt that they had an understanding. They were comfortable together and there was no need to entertain one another. When the plates were cleared, the dishes washed, Junko ran the bath water. '*Dozo*. The tub is filled,' she said. While Yuji soaked up to his neck in steaming water, Junko arranged the futons side by side on the *tatami*.

She was straightening the edges of a thick coverlet when she felt him behind her. The scent of soaped skin and shampooed hair came to her. She could feel his warmth. His hands slid over her hips, drew her gently to him.

He reached for the hem of her skirt and sought her bare flesh with his fingers.

Junko thought of the tub, full of hot water. Part of her wanted to step from Yuji's touch and sink in the soothing water. If she waited too long, it would cool, and she would have to drain it. But she could not bring herself to deny him. He was a good man, after all.

Junko turned into his embrace with eyes closed. She breathed in sharply when his lips brushed her neck. She reached for the light cord and yanked them into darkness. Their knees crumpled. They fell onto the futon.

Junko tried to imagine a baby, but a picture of Akira jumped into her mind. Akira's thick caterpillar eyebrows, his sharp cheekbones, his Western-movie-star eyes. She felt Akira's fingers gliding over her skin like water spiders. And then she opened her eyes to make the vision go away. In the dim light from the hallway, she could see Yuji's broad face. His eyes were clenched shut and she knew that he was deep in pleasure.

Long after he had rolled away from her and begun snoring softly, Junko lay awake, staring into the darkness. She thought of Emi, who was a Christian. Emi had told Junko that if she wanted a baby, she should pray to God. 'He could make miracles happen,' she said. Emi told her about the Virgin birth and a barren woman named Elizabeth who had borne a son in her old age. Junko lay in the dark with her hands pressed to her womb, listening to the boats of eel fishermen manoeuvring on the river.

When she finally fell asleep, she dreamed of Akira and she woke up feeling sick. He was like a demon, always haunting her. She'd thought that in quitting her job she was putting him behind her, but the memories were neon bright.

She wanted to forget that evening two months ago when they had found themselves alone together. She remembered glancing across the office at Akira who was looking tired with his tie askew. He rarely flirted with her the way that he did with the younger women in the office. He had never said anything about her face or perfume or what she did on Friday nights. He had never addressed her by a nickname as he did the unmarried women in their short skirts and imported make-up. Junko thought that she meant little more to him than tea cups on a tray.

But on that night, he looked away from his computer screen to her face. She was the only one left in the office, the remainder of his audience. He smiled. 'You must be tired. Your husband must be waiting for you.'

Junko shook her head. 'No, he's in Tokyo on business. He won't be back till Saturday.' She had been planning on eating leftover stew and watching a new TV drama, then going to bed, but Akira said, 'Well, then let me treat you. A little thanks for all your hard work.'

She knew that he worked late almost every night and she wondered how often he ate alone in the office. 'That would be nice,' she said. 'I don't feel like cooking.'

They went to a coffee shop since most of the other restaurants in town were closed for the night. Junko ordered curried rice and coffee and they chatted like old friends. He told her about his family.

'My daughter is going to cram school now,' he said. 'It's costing me a fortune. No more pachinko, no more mahjong.'

Junko wasn't interested in his gambling habits, but at the mention of his children she felt an ache at her core. It began growing, seeping through her veins like an insidious disease. Then she saw that an eyelash had snagged on Akira's cheek. Almost on impulse, she reached across the table and brushed it away. Something stirred within her. She began to think of possibility and the pain subsided just a little. That was two months ago.

In the morning, Junko rolled back the coverlet and rushed to the bathroom. She vomited into the sink.

'Are you all right?' Yuji asked from the other side of the door.

Junko felt her insides freeze. 'A little touch of the flu, I think.' She studied her face in the mirror—her pallor etched with lines.

'Do you want me to take you to the doctor?'

Junko felt a surge of tenderness. 'No, it's nothing serious. I'll go by myself.' She splashed cool water on her face and patted her skin dry with a towel. When she opened the door she found him still standing there and touched his arm. 'Don't worry,' she whispered. 'I'm fine.'

Her stomach was calm for the moment, so she dressed quickly and began preparing breakfast. Yuji hovered behind her, too distracted to read the morning newspaper.

They ate miso soup, rice, and poached eggs. Then Junko handed Yuji the boxed lunch she had prepared for him and followed him to the door. Their lips met. He went out after a final searching look at her face.

Junko had been to the doctor the day before. He confirmed that her wishful thinking was more than that. She would tell Yuji soon.

First, she had something important to do. After cleaning up the breakfast dishes, she went to the room where the dolls were displayed. 'It's time for you to go,' she told them. She reached for one of the ladies-in-waiting, stroked its sleeve, and sighed. Ducks settled on the river outside.

Junko began plucking the dolls, one by one, from the tiered stand and returning them to their box. She worked quietly and when the carton was full, she carried it to the door. There were no boys tossing stones from the riverbank this early in the morning. The eel fishermen had all gone home. The water rushed by, dragging pieces of wood and clots of leaves. Farther out, fish broke through the river's surface at intervals and leapt into the air. A few cars zoomed over the bridge. Junko's heart pounded as she stood there, waiting for silence. When it came, she opened the box.

She pulled out the archer and held him in her hands. Closing her eyes, she rubbed the hard plastic skin of the doll. Images flashed—Akira's fingers tearing at her blouse buttons, his breath on her neck, the jangle of his belt buckle as it hit the floor. Junko shuddered and opened her eyes. With a small cry, she hurled the doll into the stream. The little head bobbed in the current but didn't sink. The wrecked silk costume caught a ray of sun and the doll was as bright, for a moment, as the emperor's carp. Junko watched the figure until it floated out of view, then reached for another. Her fingers caressed the face of the court jester as she remembered Yuji's just-home-from-Tokyo face and her own mumbled lies.

Then, the doll was airborne and afloat. The carefully coifed lady-in-waiting flew away with the run in Junko's stockings, the court musician with tongue tracks on her skin. The dolls flowed towards the sea, cleansed by the river's water, innocent.

When the box was emptied, Junko lifted it and found that it was as light as her heart.

'It's a miracle,' she would tell Yuji that night. And she hoped he would believe her.

Lessons

Simone paused in front of a mirror before heading to class. She saw a young woman dressed for success in a tailored suit with her hair pulled back schoolmarm-style—the picture of authority. Bracing her shoulders, she vowed that tonight her students would not run rampant. Tonight, she would allow no digressions or diversions. She would fill their heads with new vocabulary.

Simone burst into the room and marched to the front of the class. Her students were settled in their seats expectantly, as always. She put a pile of papers and books in front of her and took a deep breath. 'Good evening!'

The eight Japanese grandmothers replied in chorus: 'Good evening!'

So far, so good. Simone smiled at the black-haired woman on her left. 'How are you, Mrs Kawasaki?'

There were titters, a rustling of notebook pages being turned. Mrs Kawasaki parroted, 'How are you?'

Simone suppressed a sigh. She smiled again and shook her head. 'No, no. It's a question. How are you?'

For almost nine months now, she'd been going through the same routine every Tuesday night. Why couldn't they remember such simple phrases? They seemed to have no concept of studying, expecting instead that a new language would be magically transferred from her native speaker's mouth to their sixty-something brains. Then again, Simone knew it was partly her own fault. If she were a good enough teacher, she would have figured out a way to make everything fun and memorable. As it was, she felt like an utter failure every time they met.

She decided to try again. 'Mrs Ono.'

'Yes?'

'How are you?'

The woman sat up straighter in her chair, puffed out her pillowy chest and said, 'I'm fine, thank you. And you?'

Simone relaxed a little. Mrs Ono was her star pupil in this class. Granted, she had learned quite a bit of English before Simone's arrival, fresh out of college with a one-year contract to teach English in rural Japan. Mrs Ono and her artist husband had lived in England for a year or two while he painted the cliffs of Dover. Mr Ono had died a few years ago. Unlike the other women who laboured in the sweet potato fields and pear orchards every day, Mrs Ono was a lady of leisure. As a well-off widow, she had plenty of time for pursuing her interests. She sometimes came to the class in a kimono, having hurried over from her traditional Japanese dance lessons. And she watched English programmes on educational television and always seemed to know what was going on in the world.

'What's new?' Simone asked, continuing the weekly routine she'd established. She knew that Mrs Ono would be prepared. Her replies often turned into show-and-tell sessions. Everyone regarded Mrs Ono and the tape recorder she'd placed next to her dictionary with anticipation.

The widow cleared her throat with a delicate cough, then said, 'Well, this morning as I was having my miso soup, I heard a bird singing in my garden. It was an *uguisu*.'

Simone nodded. 'Yes. A nightingale.'

'Have you ever heard a nightingale sing, Miss Simone?'

She wasn't sure. She could identify an owl, a mourning dove, or a whip-poor-will by sound, but she was no great ornithologist.

Mrs Ono continued, undaunted. 'I have made a recording of the bird's voice.' And with that, she pressed the 'play' button on her machine and the other women leaned forward to listen.

A sweet flutter of notes filled the room, and for a moment, Simone imagined that they were all sitting in a rose garden at dawn. The song was as lovely as the music that Mrs Kawasaki had played on the samisen a few weeks before. (Simone had been planning on drilling the future tense that evening, but when Mrs Kawasaki showed up after her music lesson, instrument in tow, the others had urged her to play.)

Now, after a few final trills, Mrs Ono stopped the tape recorder. The others nodded their dark heads in admiration.

Simone wondered if they were jealous of the cultured woman's extravagant lifestyle. While she roamed her garden in a silk dressing gown, the rest of them were no doubt already at work in the fields, digging up sweet potatoes or pollinating pear trees.

Having completed her presentation, Mrs Ono turned to Mrs Furukawa and said, 'How are you?' With a little whispered coaching from her inquisitor, the farm wife made it through the question. Then, she reached under the table and produced a cloth-covered basket. Reading from her notebook, she said, 'Let's enjoy sweet potatoes.'

Murmurs of pleasure rose all around. When Mrs Furukawa removed the cloth, steam curled towards the ceiling and a pleasant aroma perfumed the air.

'*Ja! O-cha o tsukurimasu!*' Mrs Kawasaki jumped up to make green tea. The other women began bustling about, helping to distribute napkins and the just-roasted sweet potatoes.

Simone sagged into her seat. *Not again*, she thought. She'd spent all afternoon preparing a grammar exercise to replace the one in the textbook that she'd deemed too difficult. Every week she laboured over her agenda, intent on teaching these ladies something, anything, before her year in Japan ended. And almost every week, it seemed, her efforts were sabotaged. The classes disintegrated into gabfests and tea parties. Worse, they were speaking in Japanese.

By now, Simone could more or less keep track of the conversation. She had picked up the news that Mrs Furukawa's son was studying in Texas, that Mrs Ono's daughter was trying to get pregnant, that Mrs Kawasaki's husband had liver problems. *But that doesn't matter*, she thought, watching her control evaporate. This was supposed to be Beginner's English. She was their teacher. They were the students. And now they were drinking tea.

Simone had other classes that she actually enjoyed teaching. In the kindergarten class, children were now reading words like 'octopus' and 'rabbit'. And in the class for businessmen, her students were able to rattle off detailed accounts of trips abroad. Even this class, composed solely of older women, had started off well. The ladies had enjoyed her slides of Charleston, the Bingo games, and charades, but she'd run out of ideas. They made no progress and they'd already covered the same basic greetings countless times. Simone was relieved that she would only be meeting with them once more.

She cast a baleful look at the grammar prints and decided to assign them as homework. Then she accepted a cup of tea from Mrs Kawasaki and bit into the soft yellow tuber. 'Delicious!' she proclaimed. The ladies giggled behind weathered hands. They didn't understand the word, but Simone felt the sentiment had been conveyed.

When they finished eating, Mrs Furukawa handed Simone a bag full of sweet potatoes. Their maroon skins had been scrubbed and they looked ready for market. 'For you, Teacher,' she said.

Did this woman understand that she lived alone? She was leaving Japan in only a few weeks and there was no way she could possibly eat all of the potatoes. Still, it would be rude to refuse, so she accepted the gift.

'Cooking? You know?' The older woman mimed boiling water, '*potsu potsu*', and shook her hand vigorously as if she were adding salt.

Simone nodded. '*Wakarimashita*. I understand. Thank you.'

Then, Mrs Sato, who almost never said a word in class and always balked at Pictionary, went up to the board and sketched out a detailed diagram for making something called 'college potatoes'. Next, Mrs Ono described a recipe for sweet potato soup that she'd picked up in her travels. And then there was no more time.

The clock chimed signalling the end of class. Simone stood and showed the papers to her students. 'Please do these as homework.'

The women waved their hands in protest. 'No, no,' Mrs Furukawa said. 'Next week is goodbye party for Miss Simone.'

'Leave everything to us,' Mrs Ono said with a smile.

Simone was glad that she wouldn't have to endure another evening of pedagogic failure. She nodded in agreement and cheerfully shooed them homewards.

The next morning when Simone ambled into the kitchen of her tiny apartment for coffee, she saw the bag of sweet potatoes on the table where she'd left them the night before. Her stomach growled with hunger and she remembered the candied yams on her plate at Thanksgiving and the spiced pies her mother sometimes made to end autumn meals. Yes, that's it! She would make a pie for her evening class. The harried businessmen who gathered on Wednesday evening were diligent students and they deserved a small, sweet reward.

After breakfast and a trip to the grocery store, she set to work. With a paring knife, she peeled the sweet potato skins in long reddish strips. She chopped the yellow meat of the vegetables and put them in a pot to boil. Then she created a small blizzard when she dumped flour into a bowl. Her hair was dusted white, but she didn't care. This would be the best pie she'd ever made.

Her apartment was soon scented with cinnamon and cloves. She opened her window to share the sensation with her neighbours. The businessmen would be so surprised. She imagined Mr Takai dashing off to brew tea and giggled.

The pie had cooled by the time Simone dressed for her evening class. She wrapped it in a *furoshiki* as Mrs Furukawa had once demonstrated. The indigo-dyed cloth had been Simone's birthday present from the class.

When she arrived at the classroom ten minutes before starting time, the room was bare. Most of the students breezed in at the sound of the chime, lugging briefcases and laptop computers. They were always in suits and ties, having come directly from work. All but one were employed by the nationally famous pharmaceutical company headquartered nearby. Mr Nakano often gave her samples of new products, such as vitamin drinks and chocolate bars for dieting. Simone had a case of after-sports massage cream in her apartment, courtesy of Mr Takai.

She put the pie on a table in the corner and settled down to wait. Mr Nakano arrived first. His hair was mussed and she imagined him tugging on locks during a tense phone call. He nodded to her—four quick, jerky nods. She wondered if he'd overdosed on caffeine. While he sat arranging papers with fierce concentration, three more class members strode in. When they were seated, Simone stood and said, 'Good evening.'

Just then the door flew open and a breathless Mr Takai burst into the room. 'Sorry to be late.' He gasped. 'I just got back from Hong Kong.'

Simone was amazed by their devotion. They came with fevers and colds. They missed out on important family events to be there. Once, in the middle of a typhoon, Mr Takai had waited outside for an hour, not knowing that class had been cancelled.

'Busy, busy, busy,' he now murmured, taking off his trench coat.

Simone cleared her throat and addressed the class. 'Tonight we are doing role plays. We will pretend that a delegation—'

The youngest student, a bespectacled lavender-suited bachelor, raised his hand. 'A what?'

Simone wrote 'delegation' on the board. Everyone immediately opened notebooks and scribbled the word down.

'A delegation of American businessmen is visiting your company for the first time. Mr Takai, Mr Kondo, and I will be the Americans. The rest of you will be Japanese.'

A wave of confusion passed over their faces, but soon subsided. They nodded eagerly, ready to attack any task set before them. Simone felt a surge of pride.

After some whispered preparations, they were ready to begin.

'Welcome to our company,' Mr Nakano said. 'How about a cup of coffee?'

Simone nodded. She'd taught them that Americans preferred to be offered food or drink as opposed to having it set before them. And she'd also taught them that it was not impolite to reply frankly in such situations.

'Yes, please,' Mr Kondo said.

'No, thank you.' Mr Takai waved his hand in front of his face. 'I don't like coffee.'

'How about tea? Juice? Beer?'

Simone shook her head and made an X with her arms. 'No beer!'

'Just kidding!' Mr Nakano laughed at his own attempt at humour. Then he nodded at the lavender-suited Mr Hayashi. The younger man ducked out of the circle of men and mimed pouring coffee. He returned to the cluster carrying a phantom tray.

'This is our office lady, Miss Hayashi,' Mr Nakano said to the 'Americans'. 'Isn't she pretty? Ha ha.'

Simone frowned. She'd explained about sexual harassment. Women in the office, she'd told them, were more than mere décor. Then again, maybe Mr Nakano was kidding again. They all seemed to be having fun. And they were speaking in English. She allowed the drama to continue without interruption.

Mr Nakano was beginning to propose a company tour when something buzzed . . . brrring! Action froze. The sound was coming from Mr Kondo's pocket. He yanked a cell phone from its silk-lined nest and spoke into the receiver, '*Moshi moshi.*' He rose from his seat and began backing to the door, bowing apologies as he went.

'Well,' Simone said brightly. 'Where were we?'

After everyone had had a chance to play a variety of roles, Simone wrote the new vocabulary on the board: negotiate, micromanagement, hostile takeover. Five minutes of class time remained.

Simone went to the table in the corner of the room and picked up the pie. She had draped the furoshiki over the pan to ensure surprise. Now, she carried the cloth-covered pan to the front of the class.

'Everyone,' she began, 'tonight I have a special treat for you.'

'Beer?' joked Mr Nakano. A few men chortled.

'No, not beer. Sweet potato pie!' And with that, Simone unveiled her masterpiece. She stood there smiling, anticipating their delight. After all, how often did these men have a chance to savour homemade American pie? 'How about a piece?'

The men stared, seemingly dumbfounded. Evidently, they were unaccustomed to dessert. Then Mr Takai glanced at his watch. 'My wife,' he said, 'she is making dinner for me now.'

'Japanese men don't like sweets, Miss Simone,' Mr Nakano explained kindly. 'Only ladies eat pie.' Simone had a vision of her father loading his plate with chocolate cake, peach cobbler, and apple strudel. In her family it was the women who declined dessert out of fear of gaining weight.

The men began packing up their notebooks and pencils and Japanese–English dictionaries. No one seemed to notice that Simone's smile had withered and her shoulders slumped. Perhaps they'd thought her offering of pie was part of the lesson. Hadn't she told them that refusal was acceptable? She had only herself to blame for her disappointment. She stared down at the golden crust and the lightly browned centre. The chime sounded and the men filed out of the classroom. She could hear their footsteps—loud, then fading. The scent of cinnamon and cloves wafted up to her, bringing little comfort.

'Miss Simone?'

She looked up, at last, into the smooth-skinned face of Mr Hayashi. They were alone in the room. 'Yes?'

'May I have a piece of pie?'

Simone fought the urge to embrace him and went for the forks.

A week later, farm women, artist's widow, and a young foreign teacher assembled at the town hall where they normally studied. This time, however, they did not enter the classroom but proceeded to a nearby restaurant that specialized in fish for the goodbye party they'd promised the week before.

Simone was dressed simply, in slacks and a sweater, but the women were decked out in their finery. Simone doubted that Mrs Furukawa had many occasions to wear that deep purple dress. And Mrs Kawasaki's golden brooch was probably kept buried deep in a drawer most of the time.

At the restaurant they were led to a private room on the second floor. Fresh flowers, artfully arranged, decorated the alcove. A table was set up at the centre of the *tatami* mats. Beer bottles stood ready, waiting to be emptied into small glasses. The first course was already laid out. In one corner there was a karaoke machine for after-dinner entertainment. They started eating after a short speech by Mrs Kawasaki.

The women came around one by one to fill Simone's glass and she returned the favour. As she sipped her beer and nibbled at sushi and pickled octopuses, she gazed around the room. Everyone was laughing and chattering, enjoying the food and the company. Simone, suffused with warmth and fellow-feeling, saw that the party was not so different from their weekly gatherings. Even in the midst of Simone's lessons on gerunds and pronouns, the women had found cause for merriment.

For so many months Simone had thought of herself as a failure. These students had not mastered even the simplest of greetings. Now, thinking of all that she had not achieved, considering her own stubborn persistence, she realized that perhaps her goals had been amiss. Her failed expectations had overshadowed smaller triumphs, moments that would later shimmer like jewels in her memory. She would treasure, most of all, Mr Hayashi's pleasure as he started on his second piece of pie, Mrs Ono's evocation of a crane as she danced before the blackboard, and the tea and sweet potatoes shared over lively conversation.

Every week her class had allowed these women to gather in the name of English. They'd had a chance to escape the families with whom they lived, ate, slept, worked, laughed, and fought nearly twenty-four hours a day. And where else would women of such disparate backgrounds—the farmers and the artist's widow—have a chance to meet and become friends? Their easy camaraderie was as good a goal as any.

When there was nothing left but fish heads and melon rinds, Mrs Ono moved to the head of the table and cleared her throat. The others fell silent and settled their hands in their laps. Simone forced her body into a kneeling position.

Mrs Ono began. 'Now I'll make a speech for Teacher.'

Simone nodded.

'First, I want to thank Miss Simone for teaching. *Kokoro kara arigato gozaimashita.* We were very poor students, but we every week looking forward to meet you. We will miss you, Simone, our American friend. Please remember us.' Mrs Ono bowed, then signalled to Mrs Furukawa, who produced an elaborately wrapped package.

'*Puresento* for you,' Mrs Furukawa said. There were tears in her eyes.

Simone reached out with both hands to take the package. A lump had formed in her throat, making words impossible. She could only smile and bow deeply.

After the party, Simone walked home under the glittering sky with the still-wrapped gift in her arms. The box was large and probably contained something fragile—a pottery vase or a doll in kimono. She wouldn't be able to stuff it into her half-packed suitcase or under an airplane seat. Well, there would be plenty of time to worry about that later. For now, she wanted to savour the lingering glow of the evening.

Much later, when the moon had faded into dawn, a sweetly familiar sound filtered into Simone's dreams. She opened her eyes and listened. A bird was serenading outside her window, singing her out of sleep. A nightingale! She pushed back her futon and rose quickly. She couldn't wait to tell Mrs Ono.

The Snow Woman

'Can you keep up, Mari-chan?' My mother stopped and looked behind her. 'Or do you want Daddy to carry you?'

I took a few more steps up Mount Tsurugi and paused to catch my breath. 'I can walk by myself.'

She smiled then, and her face became a golden moon. 'That's my girl. Pretty soon you'll be big enough to climb along with me.'

As I scuffed through dry leaves, I was ever mindful of the creatures that lurked in the underbrush, the squirrels and trickster foxes, but I kept my eyes on her backpack—a target forever out of reach. Finally, with one long upward stride, Dad was beside me, and he held my hand the rest of the way.

My mother climbed mountains. She had six yards of rope, crampons, thick-soled boots, and an axe to drive into the ice. She went away and sent back postcards of Sherpas and shaggy Kashmir goats. While other children were learning the names of imaginary countries—Narnia, Oz, Lilliput—I was memorizing mountains. I had a map on the wall of my room and each time my mother went away, I pushed another ball-headed pin into the flat peaks:

Fuji, Kilimanjaro, Denali. And then later, Annapurna and Everest.

As we climbed Mount Tsurugi, Mom's backpack loaded with books for weight and mine with just a few rice balls, I entertained myself with folk tales remembered from bedtime readings. My favourites were 'The Romance of the Milky Way' and the story of the boy who rode on the back of a turtle. But the one my mother told over and over was about a woman who lived in the mountains—the Snow Woman. When she told me that story, her arms became icy, and her eyes glittered upon some image that only she could see.

'I saw her once,' my mother said. 'Her face was exquisite—skin as white as a dragon's bones, and her lips were cherry-blossom pink.'

Then she explained how oxygen became thin high up in the mountains and the mind played tricks. One of her companions had seen not the Snow Woman but a chalet with smoke curling from its chimney, and she had conjured hot cocoa fifty yards away.

I knew that it was not really the Snow Woman my mother had seen. Anyone who looked at the Snow Woman's face would die, and my mother was still alive. Even so, I shuddered whenever I thought of their meeting on the mountain.

Here, then, is the story of the Snow Woman.

Once upon a time, there lived a pair of hunters in the mountains. They were father and son, and every day they went out together with their rifles to hunt birds, deer, and other animals. They always hunted close to home in familiar territory.

One winter's day, prey was elusive, and so they ventured farther and farther afield until they were lost. Was their home this way or that way? Snow had begun to fall, and their footsteps were obscured. Night was coming on fast, so they decided to search for lodging. They trudged and trudged until at last the son saw a light shining through the snowflakes swirling around them.

'Father!' the son cried. 'A house! Perhaps we can stay there for the night.'

His father agreed, so they travelled the short space and arrived at a simple wooden dwelling. The father knocked at the door, and after some time a young woman appeared.

'We are lost and it is cold outside. Could you, kind maiden, please put us up for the night?'

'Come in, come in. You are welcome to stay here,' she replied. And so father and son partook of a warm meal. Afterwards, the three snuggled under futons to sleep.

In the middle of the night, the son suddenly awoke.

In the dim light of the moon, he saw the young woman's radiant figure looming over him. Her eyes flashed like sun-struck diamonds. Nearby, his father appeared shrunken and still.

'Who are you?' the young man asked. His voice was as trembly as his limbs. 'What have you done to my father?'

'I am the Snow Woman,' she roared. 'I have taken your father's life. You are young, however, so I will spare you—under one condition. You must promise never to breathe a word about me to anyone. If you speak of me again, you will die!'

What choice did he have? He made his promise and fled into the blizzard outside. Finding his way back to the house he'd lived in with his father, he warmed himself by the fire.

Months passed. Little by little the snow melted. The young man hunted each day as he used to and returned each evening to a quiet and lonely house. Then one day he decided that it was time to make an offering to his father's spirit, so he set out to the mountains where he had last seen the old man. On the way he met a beautiful young woman.

There was something familiar about her, but he couldn't quite place it. Was it the blossom-strewn kimono she wore? Or the lustrous hair piled high on her head? Or was it the sweet bud of a mouth that he seemed to recall? At any rate, he couldn't stop looking at her. He fell in love.

'Kind maiden, I am but a poor and lonely hunter, but if you would have me as your husband, I'd like to make you my wife.'

She blushed and swept her gaze over the dewy grass. 'I will be your wife, Sir.'

And so they were married. Although from time to time the young man tried to remember where he had seen this woman before, he could not, and he did not let himself be bothered by this failure of memory. They had a child and lived happily in the house he had shared with his father.

This is where I wanted the story to end—with the family all together, father, mother, and child, just like we were on that day, picnicking on Mount Tsurugi.

My parents fell in love at the base of the highest mountain in the world. Dad was a member of the Peace Corps. He'd come all the way from Michigan to teach Nepalese children English. During a school break he went sightseeing with his brand-new camera. He took pictures of the women in their brightly coloured embroidered skirts, the Sherpas with their sun-ripened faces, the mountains that ranged across the sky.

I've seen his photos. If I stare at them long enough, I can jump through space and time and land at the foot of that mountain.

'Would you mind if I take your picture?' My father, then twenty-two years old, steps up to a group of climbers fitted out in parkas and locally knitted caps.

The leader, a bearded man with round glaring goggles, smiles broadly. 'Round up, gang! This young man's going to immortalize you!'

The others laugh, press closely together, and sling arms over shoulders. At the centre of them all is a woman so beautiful that she glows. It's as if there's a halo over her dark head.

When the formation breaks apart, he moves in for a closer look at that smooth-skinned face, those earth-coloured eyes. Her teeth are brighter than the snow.

'I'm Bill,' he says.

'I'm Kyoko.' And they take off their gloves to shake hands.

'When you come back down, will you have a beer with me?'

'Yes,' she says. And that's how it begins.

That expedition was not a success. A sudden snowstorm at 20,000 feet forced my mother's group to abandon their quest. My pale-haired father was waiting. He nursed my mother through her grand disappointment and followed her back to Japan.

My mother brought my father to the house she'd lived in all her life. The simple wooden structure on the edge of a sweet potato field had been in the family for generations, passed on from son to son. My maternal grandparents had only one child—a wild and wilful daughter.

On that first day, my grandmother laid out a feast for the guest: red snapper from the straits of Naruto, pickled seaweed, sweet red beans, rare pine mushrooms floating in soup, and a steak because he was American. My grandparents, my mother, and my father sipped tea and sake until late into the night.

My father believed that such hospitality was an auspicious beginning. He misunderstood the farm couple's cool formality. And so he was stunned when my grandfather took him aside the next morning and said, 'You will not marry my daughter.'

Perhaps in time my mother's parents would have relented. They had dreamed of a native son for their girl, a traditional young man who would till their fields, take over as head of the household, and provide for them in their old age. After they had recovered from the shock of this wiry, bleached-skinned stranger, after they had gotten to know his kind and generous heart, they might have softened.

My parents, however, did not wait for permission. They eloped the next day to the American consulate, and my mother's name was erased from the family registry. My grandparents disowned us all. They could not forgive the betrayal.

Living in my mother's hometown was as close as my father could get to her. If he couldn't be by her side (and he couldn't—he was a poet, not a climber), he would breathe the air that had passed through her lungs, walk the streets where her feet had stepped, live among the people who remembered the day of her birth.

It didn't matter that my grandparents wouldn't see us—the barbarian foreigner and the half-breed daughter. We had few guests because my father could not communicate with the villagers well, and the children pelted me with pebbles because I was different.

And so it was just the two of us most of the time. On my first day of *yochien*, Dad led me by the hand and delivered me to the care of my teacher. I listened to my father's stop-start Japanese and Miss Nakagawa's broken bits of English, and I wondered if they understood each other at all.

'Is your mother ill?' she asked me after my father had left.

'No,' I said. 'She's in Tibet.'

By the time she came back, I had grown two centimetres.

During her homecoming dinner, my mother was flush from her triumph of Mount Cho Oyu. We sat around the table with our bowls of delicious beef stew, but the mere sight of her blocked out all other senses. I pretended that night that we were a regular family having an ordinary dinner.

'Your father is the only one who would have me,' Mom said. 'All the other men before him wanted a stay-at-home wife who'd cook miso soup every morning.'

I looked down into my bowl. That's what I wanted too.

Dad reached across the table and clasped her hand. They gazed into each other's eyes and forgot that I was there.

It took twelve years for my mother to get her second chance at climbing Mount Everest. In the meantime she trained on the lesser mountains of Asia and wrote letters asking for funding. At last the money came through—a sponsorship from a large sporting goods company. All she had to do was plant a small flag bearing the company logo at the top of the mountain and have her picture taken alongside it. The cast and crew of this dazzling adventure were assembled. Mom started to pack.

I sat on the edge of her bed while she layered long underwear and fleece pullovers into her duffel bag. Most of the stuff would be left at the base camp, she explained. And she would need something special to wear to celebrate, perhaps in a bar in Kathmandu, thus the angora sweater dress. She showed me the locket with the picture of our family that she would wear against her heart.

Excitement coloured her cheeks as if she were already outdoors. I had a lump in my throat and my stomach was going through a spin cycle. I didn't know how to beg her to stay. I didn't tell her that I needed her around to give me advice about boys and friends and fixing my hair.

'You know, the first woman to climb to the top of Mount Everest was Japanese,' Mom said.

So what? I wanted to scream. But her words filled me with anxiety. I knew about that woman. It hadn't been easy for her. On the ascent she was buried in an avalanche and lost consciousness for six minutes. Later she told reporters that thoughts of her three-year-old daughter made her fight to stay alive. When the Sherpas dug her out from under the snow, she went to the summit.

'The Nepalese,' Mom said, 'believe that an abominable snowman lives in the mountains.' This sounded like another story, so I settled in to listen. 'The guides make an offering to the spirit of the mountain before a climb. They are very superstitious.' She laughed.

My mother was not superstitious at all. She believed in the force of nature and her own strength and will. I had never seen her pray.

On the day after her departure, I stopped by a shrine on the way home from school. I knew that there were different shrines for different wishes and I hoped that the deity with the dog statues would help me. I lit incense and wrote my prayer on a slip of paper. Then I tied the paper to the branch of a tree and begged the stone dogs to bring my mother back safely.

I found out later that the dog was the guardian spirit of pregnant women. My prayers, then, had been misdirected.

The accident was all over the newspapers, the TV, the weekly magazines. Reporters jabbed microphones at us every time we tried to leave the house. I didn't go to school. I wanted to make my mind go blank, but I was sometimes ensnared by the blue glow of the television broadcasts.

There was my mother in a pre-climb interview: 'We have state-of-the-art equipment, an experienced guide, even a satellite telephone. I have the utmost confidence that we will succeed.'

They almost did.

The producers had added menacing music, making the tragedy seem like some cheap TV drama. I saw a survivor with ice-encrusted whiskers. He moved in a daze as if he'd been dragged from a nightmare.

They got lost in a blizzard on South Col—seven of them. Two made it back to base camp, barely alive. My mother was found on her back, her coat unzipped, her eyes aimed at the sky. She'd been headed in the wrong direction—up the mountain instead of down. The television reporter said that she had frozen to death in the night.

It was not humanly possible, the reporter said, to bring back all of the bodies. There was not enough oxygen at that level to sustain such an effort. The body has its limits. It breaks. It freezes.

First, there was a phone call. And then, a week later, a knock on the door. My father answered. I was right behind him as the knob twisted in his hand. The wind funnelled in and brushed my face. A man was standing there. He had long blond hair gathered in a ponytail. The skin on his face was red and peeling as if he'd scrubbed it with steel wool. High on one cheek was a white patch that I recognized as frostbite. He was holding my mother's duffel bag.

'I'm so sorry,' he said. His voice was rusty as if he'd been wailing all day.

My father stepped back and the man stumbled into our living room, into my father's arms. I watched them from a corner—two grown men sobbing together. I myself didn't cry.

The man's name was Nick. He had been the leader of the expedition my mother had joined. Although he had reached the summit of Everest six times, there was no guarantee, he said, that a climber would make it back down.

When he settled on the sofa, a cup of coffee warming his palms, he began to tell the story that I did not want to hear.

I ran off to my room. No one tried to stop me or called me back. I fell across the bed and punched the pillows, pretending that I was boxing her. Why did she leave us? Why did she love mountains more than her daughter? Why did she favour cold wind over the warm embrace of my father?

A year later we moved to Iowa. There were no mountains in that place, only cornfields and highways that stretched forever. Dad got a job teaching English literature to high schoolers. He remarried not long after that. My stepmother looked nothing like Mom, nothing like me. I was exotic in that town of beef-and-corn-fed farm children, and boys wrote me love poems that they called haiku. My stepmother taught me how to bake bread and shave my legs. She went over my homework with me until the last day of high school.

The evening before my graduation, I ironed my white ruffled dress and hung it on my closet door. Then I sank down to the floor and stared at the carpet. Dad found me like that.

'What's wrong?' he asked.

I shrugged. 'I miss her. I wish she were here to see me graduate.'

He nodded. He missed her too.

'Why did she have to climb those stupid mountains anyhow? I mean, what was the point?'

Dad sat down beside me and pulled me against his chest. I could feel the steady thump of his heart. 'She was special, your mother. She had big dreams.'

I couldn't help remembering a time when she had stayed with us for months on end, when she had sat by the window, staring outside. Some days, she didn't even get out of bed. She wasn't good at cooking or cleaning, or maybe she didn't even try. Maybe she wouldn't have survived without her ambitions. Maybe that's all that had kept her going.

He spoke softly in his velvet-rubbed voice. His arms held me tight. I knew that I didn't have to be strong for him any longer and I undammed a river of tears.

That night I dreamed of the Snow Woman. In the dream, I was in Michigan, visiting my paternal grandparents a few days before Christmas. I took the sled with iron runners that my father had glided on as a boy out to the front lawn. The lawn had a slope, which made it perfect for a little girl's sledge ride. I was bundled up in a plush hooded coat, my mittens on a string, a stocking cap with a bobble on top. Around me there was nothing but snow. I threw myself face down on the sledge and shoved off with my booted foot. The sled went flying, and I could feel the sting of wind in my eyes. Suddenly, a great being rose in front of me. It was a woman—but a giant woman. Her hair fanned out like the sketchy branches of winter trees. Her long gown was an icy blue, and pale hands reached from the loose sleeves. I tried to scream, yell for my father to rescue me, but my lungs were frozen in fear. And then I looked up, into the face of that mythic creature, and saw that it was my mother.

Here is how the story ends.

One evening after the child had been put to bed, the hunter and his wife were seated around the charcoal brazier. The young man was weaving rope from rice straw, and the wife was mending the sleeve of a kimono. Once again, the man had the feeling that he had seen this woman before their marriage. He wondered aloud where they had first met.

'What are you talking about, you silly!' his wife chided.

Just then, the embers flared up, and the flash of fire seemed to ignite her eyes. He saw her eyes sparkle like sun-struck diamonds and he remembered.

'I know!' he shouted. 'You're the Snow Woman!'

She turned to him with a sudden fury. 'You have broken our promise!' She rose over him, frozen tears falling from her eyes.

Although the Snow Woman had vowed to take the life of the man if he ever spoke of her true identity again, she had grown to love him and their child. She could not bear to harm either of them. For this reason, she could not stay. With a great howl, she blew out the door and into the night, and they never saw her again.

In midwinter, when snowflakes dance in the wind and grey clouds darken the sky, the man and his child warm themselves with memories of having loved her.

A Real Job

You're ready for a real job. For the past fifteen years, you've been fitting in random part-time gigs while raising your multiply-disabled child, supplementing your Japanese husband's salary as a high school P.E. teacher. But now, you've had enough of reading *Everyone Poops* to preschoolers, enough of kindergartners groping you during 'London Bridge is Falling Down', enough of sullen businessmen forced to study English after hours in a company class. You've had enough of scrounging between the sofa cushions for one hundred yen coins and tofu (only eighty-eight yen per pack!) for dinner. Enough of your husband saying, 'Don't you think it's time to go back to work?'

When your Canadian friend who teaches full-time at the local university tells you about an opening—instructor of American Culture—you immediately update your résumé. And why not? You're American, after all. Between driving your kid to Deaf School and physical therapy, between once-a-week kindergarten classes and twice-a-week businessmen, you've managed to write and publish seven books. You have a master's degree from a prestigious American university. You know all about Lady Gaga.

You submit your application with a week to spare before the deadline.

Your husband buys a bottle of wine. 'I have a good feeling about this,' he says.

Although a celebration is premature, you drink the wine together. You wait. A week passes, then two weeks. The phone doesn't ring. No one from the university sends email. Finally, you get an official-looking letter in the mail, along with a package containing your seven books and various other publications. 'We regret to inform you that . . .'

Your Canadian friend tells you that someone else was hired for the position—a guy from Jordan who wrote a book in Japanese on the US government's complicity in the events of 9/11.

'Sorry,' she says, and you can tell by her pained expression that she really is sorry. 'I'll let you know when something else comes up.'

A year later, you publish your eighth novel, but the advance is small, hardly enough to cover the cost of a new wheelchair for your daughter. Your house is falling into disrepair. Paint is peeling, the tatami mats are musty. Your husband keeps saying, 'Why don't you get a full-time job?' but there are just so many things that you can do as a middle-aged American woman in rural Japan. You keep reading *Everyone Poops*. You keep playing Duck, Duck, Goose. You scour online job listings every day.

One day, you and your Canadian friend are having lunch at Starbucks (her treat, because this is something that you really can't afford).

'You know that Jordanian guy we hired?' she asks before taking a sip from her matcha latte.

'Yeah, what about him?'

'Well, a couple of weeks ago he announced that he is no longer going to teach American Culture.'

'Can he do that?'

She nods. 'He has tenure.'

'So what's he going to teach instead?'

'Well, he put a new sign on his door. Now he's teaching Islamic Studies.'

'Huh.' Maybe that's what the university wanted all along. Who knows how these people think?

'But there's an opening in the Literature Department,' she tells you. 'One of my colleagues is going on maternity leave. You'd be perfect for that.'

You *would* be perfect. You majored in literature in college, and you've written several works of literary fiction yourself. Those books may not be bestsellers, but you've won prizes and starred reviews. Although you've heard that foreigners are rarely given jobs teaching literature in Japan, and are usually consigned to teaching English conversation to freshmen, it's worth a shot. This time, you prepare your resume on expensive vellum paper. To compensate, you'll be eating tofu twice this week.

This time, your husband doesn't buy wine. He's become more cautious, more crafty. 'You need a connection,' he says. 'That's how things work in Japan. If you don't become friends with the right people, you'll never get a job.'

You mention your Canadian friend. She's a well-liked insider with tenure. And you know a couple of other people who work there—a guy from Uganda and a few part-time workers from various countries.

He shakes his head. 'Foreigners don't count. It has to be a Japanese person.'

A couple of weeks later, your books come back in the mail, along with a letter: 'We regret to inform you . . .'

You're not terribly surprised.

'I didn't get the job,' you tell your Canadian friend the next time you meet for coffee.

'I'm so sorry,' she says. 'I put in a good word for you. I told the chairman about your books and your literary awards, but . . .'

'So who got it?'

'This German guy. He's been working in a contract position.'

'A German. Huh. And he's going to teach American Literature?'

She waves her hand dismissively. 'He wrote his master's thesis on superheroes in American comics. I think his specialty is *The Incredible Hulk*.'

'Well, I bet the students will enjoy his class,' you say, trying not to sulk. They'll probably enjoy comics more than the Fitzgerald novel you fantasized about teaching.

'Maybe they were intimidated by him,' she says. 'He has gangster tattoos and he's always yelling at people. Maybe they were afraid of what he'd do if they didn't hire him.'

You're not a yeller. After sixteen years of being mother to a child with special needs, you've developed reservoirs of patience. All these years in Japan have changed you. Your street smarts have atrophied. You speak too softly and apologize too much. And now you're not tough enough even for rural Japan.

'On the plus side, there's another opening,' your friend says.

'There is?'

'They're looking for someone to fill the contract position. It's not tenured, but it's full time.'

You're already exhausted with this whole job-hunting business, but you made too much money in your part-time gigs to remain on your husband's health insurance. Now, not only do you have to pay income tax and cover your own pension, you also have to use your meagre earnings to pay for obligatory national health insurance. You are now working more but making even less money than before. How is that possible? You can't figure it out. Obviously, you have no future in the mathematics field.

You send in your application again, printing your resume on recycled paper. This time, you send only three of your eight published books and a handful of articles and book reviews, not all one hundred of them. None of that stuff seems to have impressed them before, so why bother?

To your amazement, you're called in for an interview. You buy a black suit and a white blouse. You take special care with your make-up. When you arrive at the room where the interview is held, several professors are seated already in a row of chairs. One of them, an older gentleman, says, 'I know your husband. We sometimes go drinking together.'

'Oh, really?' What else can you say to something like that?

Everyone asks a question. They want to know how you will improve students' TOEIC (Test of English for International Communication) scores and whether or not you are planning on pursuing your doctorate degree. One person asks you to name your favourite Japanese writer. '*Is this relevant?*' you want to ask. Instead, you cast about for a safe answer and come up with 'Natsume Soseki', even though you've never read any of his books.

When the interview is over, you pick your daughter up from Deaf School, go grocery shopping, and make dinner. When your husband comes home, he looks in the pot and frowns. 'Curry and rice again? We had it for school lunch today.'

You want to dump the pot over his head and watch the gravy slide over his face like lava, but you don't. Instead, you tell him about the interview. 'Who was that guy, anyway? The one you go drinking with?'

'He was my mentor,' your husband says. 'He was the principal at the first high school where I worked. Now he's a college professor.'

Later that evening, your husband gets a phone call. It's his mentor saying that you've got the job.

This time, you do celebrate. With champagne. And the next time you go to Starbucks with your Canadian friend, you pay for the coffee. You tell the preschoolers and businessmen that you won't be teaching them any more. The preschoolers make cards for you out of construction paper and host a little party with juice and rice crackers. Each child shares a favourite memory of your time together. The businessmen take you drinking and give you an expensive gift—a vase thrown on a wheel by a famous local potter.

Your first day on the job, you go to the main office. A secretary gives you a key. 'Your office is on the second floor of building eight. Do you know where that is?'

'Umm, I'll find it,' you say.

Inside your office there is a desk with a big box on top. You look in the box and see a computer that you have no idea how to set up.

Once you're settled in, however, you find that you enjoy the job. Your students are bright and motivated and they don't try to grope you. No one asks you to read *Everyone Poops* or explain business etiquette in South Dakota. You don't get to talk about Lady Gaga or *The Great Gatsby*, but you now have health insurance and pension payments, not to mention your own office that you decorate with plants and art. Tofu is now an optional dinner choice.

You now have to attend faculty meetings as an 'observer'. Most of the time, you are the only foreigner in the meetings, which are conducted entirely in Japanese. Most of the time, you are the only woman. During one, at which the German Associate Professor of American Literature is present, you venture to ask a simple question.

The German turns to the chairman and says, 'Is she really allowed to speak? Isn't she supposed to keep quiet?

'He's trying to pull your tail,' your husband says when he hears about the incident. It's a funny expression. You imagine that you are a monkey being yanked out of a jungle tree. But it seems as if your husband may be right. For whatever reason, your new colleague doesn't seem to like you. Suddenly, there is a savage one-star review of one of your books on Amazon.com written largely in non-native speaker English: 'The author is clearly not knowing about the Japanese tea ceremony. [. . .] This book is continuing until I feel boredom to tears,' etc. It must be him! Pulling your tail!

You try to do your job conscientiously, teaching classes that last the full ninety-minutes, making yourself available during office hours to students who want to practice speaking in English, and helping Japanese colleagues with their academic papers. You are desperate for your three-year contract to be renewed. The thought of once again having to scrounge for one hundred yen coins is enough to bring you to tears. But as you reach the end of your contract, you realize that it hasn't been enough. You have published your ninth novel and taught as many classes as were asked of you—hundreds of students every semester—but you haven't made the right connections. You've failed to impress.

Although you do your best to stay alert to potential openings, nothing comes up. You learn that an Australian guy who used to run a pizza parlour for homesick foreigners has been hired for a new position that you somehow didn't hear anything about. Apparently, this guy has had a Master's in Education all this time. Also, he has the right friends.

Your contract is dwindling. Your husband is worried. Your daughter needs a new hearing aid.

While scrolling through the job listings, you come across a full-time English teaching position at a nearby language school. Health insurance is provided, plus four weeks of vacation. There's the possibility of a promotion.

The job calls for someone with experience teaching small children, preferably a native speaker. What choice do you have? You sigh and send in your resume.

At the interview, the harried young woman who owns the school serves you tea. She doesn't ask you about methodology or how you will improve TOEIC scores. She doesn't even seem to care if you have a degree. You can hear children crying in the background.

'We're very short-staffed,' she says. 'When can you start?'

'Right away,' you tell her. In fact, you'd be happy to start immediately. You reach into your briefcase and pull out a book: *Everyone Poops*.

Julia in the Desert

Day #1

'This isn't Luxor,' Joji sneered. At sixteen, everything was beneath contempt. 'This is more like Khafre. The Sphinx is in front of Khafre.'

Julia rolled her eyes. After the short flight from Osaka and the long flight from Seoul, they were all cranky. 'This is America,' she said. 'Who cares?' She could be snarky, too, though she was secretly impressed by her son's knowledge of Egyptian archaeology. They had never been to Egypt.

It had been her husband, Yu, who'd wanted to visit Las Vegas. Julia had used it as bait, a visit to the in-laws in Ohio no longer being incentive enough to get him to hop on a plane for fourteen hours, and endure ten days of jet lag, cornflakes, and Obama-bashing. The kids, too, were starting to get blasé about travel. When she'd floated the idea of a family vacation to Italy, they'd sighed.

Marina had started signing furiously about the potential lack of Wi-Fi, while Joji had said, 'If I miss school, I won't get a certificate for perfect attendance this year.'

'Believe me,' Julia scoffed, 'in ten years—maybe even a few months from now—that won't even matter.'

School was on all the time. Even during so-called holidays, Japanese kids were rounded up for 'extra lessons' and 'summer school'. Julia was convinced that the whole system was set up to keep the young and impressionable from straying too far and developing ideas of their own. *My children are sheep! They're robots!*

The prime minister had declared that college students no longer needed to study humanities. In fact, the government didn't want them to study history and literature any more. They would be allowed to learn enough English to discuss engineering or whatever with foreigners, but they didn't need that other stuff. Oh, and the business about Japanese soldiers ransacking Nanjing and enslaving Korean women for sex? Never happened.

The kids were, let's face it, Japanese. Sure, they had American passports thanks to their American mom, but they'd been born and raised in a conservative Japanese farm town. Julia had given up on her dream of bicultural children, but it was good—necessary, even—to temper their father's increasingly nationalistic rhetoric with a little American. Julia had to get her kids out of Japan, if only for a moment, before they were totally brainwashed.

The hotel was, of course, faux Egyptian, shaped like a pyramid, but with no fewer than three Starbucks outposts inside.

Yu stood off to one side with the kids—Marina in her wheelchair and Joji slouching next to her—craning his neck towards the casino, while she checked in. The clerk appeared to be an immigrant. No one who worked in Las Vegas seemed to have been born in America.

'Does he need a roll-in shower?' the clerk asked with a nod towards Marina. Julia tried to place his accent. India?

'*She*,' Julia corrected. 'And yes, that would be nice.' That was the second time since deplaning that Marina had been mistaken for a boy. The first time had been while they were waiting to go through customs. The Filipino guy who'd been assigned to help them with the wheelchair had referred to Marina as 'him'. Julia had let it pass, thinking the mistake a result of second-language pronoun confusion. God knows her students in Japan had plenty of trouble keeping the identifiers straight. But English was the lingua franca back in India, wasn't it?

Julia glanced at her daughter as she waited for the card keys. Nothing wrong with tomboys and being transgender, but Marina was a girlie girl, a lover of all things pink and Hello Kitty. Maybe they should have let her keep her hair long. Maybe she should be wearing make-up, like her American teenaged peers, and more feminine clothes. At least then she wouldn't hear people calling her a boy. At that age, it would probably send her into despair.

'Here you are, ma'am.' The clerk slid a receipt and the card keys across the desk. Julia handed them to Yu.

'I'll meet you up at the room,' she said.

She got in another line to rent a car for their excursion to Hoover Dam three days hence. Not only would they see the Blue Man Show and Cirque de Soleil, but they'd learn some history too. Julia herself was keen to get out into the desert. She'd never been, but she'd had fantasies about wandering the sands like Gertrude Bell.

In the hotel room, the kids had already accessed the hotel Wi-Fi and were absorbed in their iPads. Due to the time difference, their friends in Japan were probably just waking up.

Yu was watching TV. Donald Trump's orange face took up half the screen before giving way to a commercial about the Miss Universe pageant about to take place in Vegas. Julia remembered that there had been a hullaballoo in Japan over Miss Japan because her father was a foreigner. Some people thought that she wasn't authentically Japanese, yet in international athletic competitions the Japanese were always proud to claim their *hafu* representatives, who, thanks to foreign genes tended to be taller and stronger than their 'whole' team members.

But who cares? For the next two weeks, they were in multicultural America. It would be good for her kids to see folks of all colours and creeds mixed up together.

'Well, why don't we go grab a bite to eat and look around?' Julia tried to infuse her voice with cheer, although what she really wanted to do was take a bath and go to bed. She never slept on airplanes. But here they were, and she was determined to make the most of it.

They had burgers in a sports bar on the first floor. The guys kept their eyes on the widescreen TV broadcasting an NBA game while Marina stole surreptitious glances at the iPad resting on her knee, checking for free Wi-Fi, no doubt.

When they returned to their room afterwards, bloated with Coke and carbs, Yu got a second wind. 'I'm gonna go try my luck at the blackjack tables. Do you want to come?'

Julia shook her head.

'Hey, Dad,' Joji said, his thumb in a guidebook. 'If you win lots of money, can we do a bungee jump from the tower?'

'Sure. And dinner at the Paris Hotel for you,' he said, winking at Julia.

'Fingers crossed,' Julia muttered. She took a scalding shower and negotiated Marina into bed. Unlike most teenagers, Joji slept according to a rigid schedule, but left to her own devices, his sister would stay up all night. She'd read that kids with cerebral palsy often had sleep issues. Something to do with the brain. The jet lag didn't help. By the time Julia had pulled the covers up to Marina's chin, Yu was back.

'Well?'

He shook his head. 'I lost three hundred dollars in twenty minutes.'

Day #2

Out of the hotel and away from the Strip, there was a string of fast-food restaurants. They had to be cheaper than the hotel restaurants.

'Why don't we try the Panda Express?' Julia asked. She was pretty sure there would be no dinner at the Paris Hotel. Yu had gambled away another fifty dollars that afternoon, this time at the slot machines.

They headed down the sidewalk, away from the gush of the Bellagio's fountain, the castle of Excalibur, towards the seedier, cheaper district. Julia pushed Marina's wheelchair, while Joji slouched along behind. She wondered if she should tell him to not wear the hood of his sweatshirt.

A guy with a droopy moustache and a green flak jacket, came dragging a wheeled carry-on bag from the opposite direction. He was ranting incoherently.

Julia stared straight ahead, intent on ignoring him, hoping her family would take the cue.

'I was going to kill somebody today,' the guy said, 'but then I saw your son.'

Julia looked over at Joji, alarmed, but the guy was pointing to Marina, the presumably inspirational-because-disabled deterrent of his violence. She couldn't help herself. 'She's my *daughter*.'

Yu touched her elbow. 'Maybe we should go across the road,' he said in a low voice.

'Yeah, okay,' Julia quickly agreed. She wondered if they should call the cops. Maybe this guy really did plan to kill someone.

The Panda Express was two doors down from a rifle range. For a fee, apparently anyone could fire a machine gun. *Welcome to America, kids! Everything you've heard is true!*

'Dad, can we?' Joji pointed to the sign. A Rambo lookalike lofted his weapon.

'No,' Julia said. 'Absolutely not.'

Day #3

Julia had bought tickets on the internet to a Cirque de Soleil show, which she now realized was a dumb idea. Booths selling discounted tickets were scattered along the Strip. They could have seen anything they wanted for half price! Well, at least they had decent seats.

The performance was as spectacular as advertised: The vertical battle scene! Bare-chested men running in hoops! The juggling! The dancing! The costumes and make-up! Julia was overwhelmed by the possibilities of the human body. Immediately after the show, Yu and the kids rushed through the gift shop as if a mask or a T-shirt could prolong the high. Plastic bags slung over their shoulders, they emerged from the hotel, back onto the Strip, into gritty real life.

A crowd had gathered down the road in front of the faux Eiffel Tower at the Paris Hotel. They heard the blare of sirens as a fleet of ambulances approached, saw the red lights of a patrol car spotlighting spectators' shocked faces.

'What happened?' Julia asked, grabbing onto Yu's shirtsleeve. Like *he* would know.

'Someone said there was a suicide bomber,' a guy nearby blurted out. He was standing on tip-toes, trying to see what was going on.

'Like a terrorist?' Joji asked. Julia thought that he sounded a little bit scared.

'Yeah, fuckin' ISIS, man,' the rubbernecker said unhelpfully.

Yu nodded as if it was all so-o-o predictable.

Way to foment hysteria, Julia thought. 'Let's move along, gang,' she said to her family. 'I'm sure there's an explanation.'

Marina wagged her finger. 'What? What?'

Julia shook her head and began pushing her wheelchair in the direction of their hotel. 'Why don't we splurge on some ice cream?' She mimed licking a cone.

Joji and Marina both nodded enthusiastically. Junk food was always a great diversion.

Back at the hotel, after gooey sundaes, they turned on CNN. Lots was happening in Vegas that night, it turned out. During the Miss Universe pageant hours earlier, the MC had named the wrong contestant as the winner. And across from the Bellagio, where they had stood watching water spurt into the sky, a woman had driven her car into a group of Canadian tourists lingering on the sidewalk. People were dead, some injured. A toddler had been in the car with her.

'Dangerous country,' Yu said, his eyes bright, as if he were watching a movie, not a report of something that had happened in real life. Everything about Vegas seemed fake.

Joji shoved in his earbuds and cracked open a textbook. Marina was already texting her friends in Japan, oblivious to the TV. Maybe they were experiencing sensory overload, Julia reasoned. Maybe Las Vegas was just too much. She thought about the stretch of pure desert beyond, an expanse of nothing but sand, tumbleweeds, jackrabbits, and cacti.

'Thank goodness we're going to see the Hoover Dam tomorrow,' Julia said.

No one seemed to be listening.

Day #4

The next morning the alarm went off at six. Julia pounded the clock with her fist and snapped on the light. The guys groaned in unison. Marina didn't stir.

'Come on! The concierge said that if we wait too long, we'll get stuck in traffic.'

'I thought we were going to go bungee jumping,' Joji mumbled.

'Did your dad win any money?' Julia poked Marina's shoulder. No response.

'No, but . . .'

'Well, then. Today is our only chance to see the great Hoover Dam. It'll be educational!' she said, eyeing the stack of textbooks beside Joji's rollaway.

'Yeah, but it won't be on the test,' Joji said. 'Why don't you go? I'll stay here.'

Julia sighed. 'Yu? Are you going to back me up here?'

'I think we should just hang out around here, maybe check out the Trump Hotel.'

'I'm absolutely not going to set foot in anything Trump!'

Yu rubbed his eyes, surprised at her outburst. 'Okay, okay.' Julia grabbed a pair of jeans and a sweater out of her suitcase and went into the bathroom to change. She figured that by the time she'd washed and creamed her face and put on her make-up, the rest of her family would have gotten out of bed. But no. They were all snoring softly.

'Hey, you guys,' she said.

Yu's eyelids flickered open.

'I'm going to see the Hoover Dam. If you're coming with me, get out of bed now. Otherwise, I'll see you at dinner.'

'Bye, Mom,' Joji said. 'Take some pictures, okay?'

Once she was behind the wheel of the rental car, Julia realized that she was not all that gung-ho on seeing the dam. She suddenly recalled that Hoover was one of the more reviled past presidents—a businessman with no previous governing experience who drove the country to the edge of ruin. Also, she dreaded the thought of being called upon to photograph families and couples as she wandered from explanatory plaque to plaque by herself. If she was going to be on her own, she'd rather be somewhere solitary. She decided that she would just get out of the city, away from the insanity of the Strip, and drive for a while.

She manoeuvred the sedan out of the parking garage and onto the street. The car was equipped with a navigation system, so she wasn't likely to get lost. When she was ready to come back, she'd just enter the hotel address and heed the computerized voice. For now, she was going to try to get someplace where there was hardly any traffic.

She drove past small businesses and houses, past the billboard welcoming visitors to Las Vegas, and continued beyond the mall. This was more like it. Okay, maybe the terrain was dull. There were no 'colourful' people or castle-shaped buildings, but it was normal. She imagined neighbourhoods of plumbers and schoolteachers and bank clerks, and their kids with their homework and baseball teams and hobbies, and their ordinary lives. She let her mind go blank. And then she found herself surrounded by desert. The rental sedan was the only car on the road for as far as she could see.

What if I drove off the road, into the desert? she wondered. Maybe she could park somewhere, and walk around barefoot in the sand, pretend to be Gertrude Bell. Her heartbeat sped up. *Why not?* She turned the wheel and left the highway, half expecting bells and alarms to go off or maybe a giant Gila monster to emerge from the sand to punish her for breaking the rules. But nothing happened. She suddenly felt liberated. She was free of the scary homeless guy, free of Miss Universe, free of her grouchy children, free of her unlucky husband, and whatever had happened to that crowd of people on the sidewalk. Behind the car, sand sprayed like surf. It was as if she were in a boat, gliding on a sugary white sea.

Okay. Here. She brought the car to a gentle halt and turned off the engine. When she stepped out of the car and looked back, she couldn't quite make out the road. How far had she come? Not all that far. And anyway, she had the navigation system. She would be able to get back, no problem.

Julia took off her shoes and dug her feet into the sand. The dirt underneath was cool. In fact, with the wind whipping around her, tossing grains into her face, it was pretty cold. She put her shoes back on and walked around the car, thinking, *I'm finally here! I'm in the desert!*

People often spoke of transformative spiritual events taking place in the desert. Jesus, for example. And others high on peyote. Julia leaned against the car, waiting for enlightenment, but she just felt cold. And a little lonely. Why hadn't she brought a notebook, at least, to record her feelings? She remembered that Joji had asked for photos. She got back in the car and rummaged around in her purse until she found her smartphone. She pressed the button on the side, but the screen remained dark. Great. The battery was dead.

Her stomach grumbled. It was lunchtime. Maybe she should find a little diner, have a sandwich, and then head back. She cranked the engine and pressed on the gas pedal. The car didn't move. Or it did, but it seemed to sink a little instead of going forward or backward. Julia suddenly realized that the car was stuck in the sand.

She tried to remember everything she knew about this situation. Could she put boards under the tires? The car mats? What would Gertrude Bell do? If only she could access YouTube. And why weren't Yu and Joji here with her? They could push the car. Why had she been so stupid as to drive off the highway anyway? In spite of the chill, beads of sweat broke out on her forehead. She wanted to cry, but what good would that do?

Julia got out of the car again and studied the tires now submerged halfway into the sand. She dug until her hands were raw, then got behind the wheel again, but no dice. She swung herself out of the car again, and popped the trunk, hoping to find a shovel or a manual on *How to Survive in the Desert* or perhaps *How to Recharge Your Smartphone Battery Without USB Cables.* All she found was a spare tire.

The wind was picking up. A tumbleweed rolled by as if on cue. She saw a cloud of sand in the distance. A tornado? Whatever it was, the thing was coming closer and closer. Julia remembered reading about sandstorms in the desert. One could be buried and suffocated. At the very least, one's hair and skin could be coated with silt. She had better get back in the car.

As she sat there on the vinyl seat contemplating her future, she wondered how long it would be before her family went for help. Would they even know who to talk to, or what to say? She'd told them that she was going to the

Hoover Dam, so officials would look there first. Ironically, she was the one who always complained that the men in her family never left notes, that they never answered their cell phones when she called, that she always had trouble finding them. Ironically, she knew where they were—on the Strip! Probably at Panda Express!—and they had no idea that she was out here, stuck in the sand.

The cloud of sand approached like a meteor hurling towards earth. This, too, seemed unreal, like a dream or a movie. Julia leaned back against the seat as if she were in a theatre. After several more minutes, she could make out movement. Legs. Lots of legs! Of horses! A herd of wild horses, churning up sand. They were coming right at her. Julia thought of the Four Horsemen of the Apocalypse. Then again, these horses didn't have any riders.

She could hear the thunder of their hooves as they came closer. She braced herself for the cracking of the windshield, the crunch of metal as these beasts trampled the vehicle or, maybe worse, the thud and fall of their bodies as they collided with the car. Suddenly, the sedan was surrounded by dust. The horses became murky ghostlike shapes shrouded in sand, parting like a sea, surrounding the car, washing past it, and then coming together again behind it.

Julia sat in the car until the air had cleared and the sand had settled. Did that really happen? Did a herd of horses really just run past the car? When she looked back, she saw no sign of the animals. She opened the door and found evidence. The horses' hooves had packed down the dirt, creating a path. The tires, Julia realized, were no longer stuck in the sand.

As she turned the key and stepped on the gas pedal, she held her breath. When the car gained traction and surged forward, she exhaled. She managed to make her way back to the highway without using the navigation system. She couldn't wait to get back to her family and tell them what had happened. *America the beautiful! That's what I'm talking about!* But even as she began to formulate the story in her head, she knew that Yu, Joji, and Marina would never believe her. She wasn't the kind of person to drive off the road and the idea of wild horses coming to her rescue was too far-fetched. Without photos, they would think she made it all up or that she was telling them about something from a Disney movie. They'd think it was fake, unreal—all smoke and mirrors and wires. Maybe she should keep it to herself. She would treasure this memory as she looked forward to a shiny new era in which a woman president would banish guns.

The Woman Who Loved Insects

Izumi had spent an hour waxing poetic about dragonflies. She'd told her students how they can migrate on gossamer wings across oceans, and how the males have a row of spikes on their front legs just for cleaning their eyes. She told them how dragonflies formed a heart as they mated in mid-air, and how they symbolized pure water to the Navajo. In Japan, of course, they represented happiness. Now, she stepped into her office and went to the window. She peered out, trying to find some dragonflies flitting through the warm afternoon air.

Students milled about in the courtyard, sipping cold canned tea and punching out text messages on their cell phones. She could easily pick out the ones engaged in mating dances—the girls who giggled from behind their palms and glanced from under bangs, the boys who affected indifference but flexed their muscles all the same. And this was odd—a lone foreign man sitting on a bench with a book. He was too old to be a student. Perhaps he was a visiting professor that she hadn't yet met. He'd probably turn up at a faculty meeting.

Izumi leaned out the window and took a deep breath. It was getting to be her favourite time of the year. Soon the air would be buzzing with the sound of insects. Crickets would chirp. Bees would hum. Mosquitoes and cicadas would add to the orchestral mix.

Ahh, summer. Izumi glanced from her desk to the calendar on the wall. She had blocked out a week for a trip to the mountains where she hoped to find a rhinoceros beetle for her studies. These days you could just walk into a department store and buy a stag beetle or a kuwagata—you could order them on the internet!—but how could you learn about the creatures' habits from that?

No, there was nothing like tramping through the woods, net propped against her shoulder, the scent of pine and grass filling her nostrils. Sometimes she invited students along. It was a joy to watch the faces of the ones who shared her passion when they finally found a black-lacquered beetle clinging to the bark of a sawtooth oak. On occasion, she'd made the mistake of inviting the less enthusiastic, the posers, who slapped away at flies and gnats as they hiked, grumbling all the while.

Someday, after she got married and became a mother, Izumi would bring her own daughter into the mountains to search for insects. Maybe they'd go on a bug safari to Brazil to hunt down the magnificent Hercules, the largest beetle of all, or to the Congo Gorilla Forest in pursuit of the Goliath beetle.

'Chirrup! Chirrup!' Izumi reached into her tote bag and fished out her cell phone. She could tell in a glance that it was her mother.

'Moshi moshi.'

'Izumi-chan, we have found the perfect man for you!'

Izumi rolled her eyes. 'Is that so?' How many times had she called up, claiming the exact same thing?

'The matchmaker said that this man has a great job with a high salary and he's very handsome. You'll be having dinner with him Saturday night.'

'Fine.' She had no plans other than watering her plants and trimming her toenails. To tell the truth, she was hoping that just once, one of these perfect men would live up to his billing. She truly did want to get married and start a family. After all, without a husband, how would the little girl of her daydreams come into being?

'Don't forget,' her mother said. 'Don't tell him about your, er, interest in bugs.'

'I won't.'

Throughout her girlhood, Izumi's mother had nudged her towards piano, ballet, and tea ceremony. Nothing, however, had captivated her as much as the six-legged creatures she found in the field. On Girl's Day, she had helped her mother set up the tiers of kimono-clad dolls representing the emperor and empress and court, but she had always been impatient to stow them away again.

'I need to put my ant farm here,' she'd said. The dolls didn't move, but the ants were endlessly industrious. She loved watching the worker ants as they tunnelled, carrying bits of food twenty times greater in weight than their tiny glossy bodies.

Izumi and Haruki, her Saturday night date, exchanged a few text messages and set up a meeting. They were modern people; they didn't need to be chaperoned by parents or the matchmaker. They arranged to meet in front of a popular Italian restaurant.

Izumi told him that she would be wearing a red dress with black dots—her ladybug dress. He told her that he would be holding a rose—a bit of a cliché, but he would be easy to find.

On Saturday night, she donned the dress, which was silk and reminded her of worms munching mulberry leaves, made up her face, and took a taxi to the restaurant. Several people were milling about the entrance, but she spotted him right away. He was taller than the others. His hair was a little long and pulled back into a stubby ponytail. She liked the hair immediately, and the cricket-black leather jacket that he wore. He was obviously different from the guys she usually encountered, who always arrived in suits and ties.

'Izumi-san,' he said, bowing slightly as she came near. 'Your dress is lovely.'

'Thank you,' she said, accepting the rose he held out to her. She brought it to her nose.

'And here is another gift,' he said, handing over a small package.

Izumi couldn't help thinking of praying mantises. During courtship, the male presented the female with a 'nuptial gift', a morsel of food. If the female did not find it to her liking, she was apt to devour her suitor.

'Shall we?' Haruki ushered her into the restaurant.

They were shown to a back booth, dimly lit by a sconce on the wall. It was all very romantic, Izumi thought, and the scent of garlic and basil from the kitchen made her mouth water.

At the table, Izumi opened her gift. It was a thin, cotton handkerchief printed with a profusion of purple blossoms. *Hydrangea*, Izumi thought. She could just about hear bees buzzing around the summer flower. The gift was lovely but useful. Also, it was not so expensive as to make her feel any obligation.

'How perfect!' she said.

They ordered plates of spaghetti and a bottle of wine.

'Please tell me, what it is you do again?' Izumi asked, twirling noodles on her fork.

'I design computer software,' Haruki said. 'I have my own company. And you? I heard you're a science teacher?'

'A professor,' Izumi said. She couldn't help herself. She was pleased to note, however, that he didn't bat an eye. Emboldened, she decided to tell him more. 'I teach courses in entomology.'

'Ahh, the study of insects,' he said, pouring more wine into her glass. 'I had a kuwagata beetle when I was a boy. I remember brushing its back to get rid of the mites. It lived for almost three years.'

'I had a kuwagata too,' Izumi said excitedly. 'And a lot of other bugs. One time, my ant farm spilled out all over the tatami. My mother was furious.'

They both laughed.

This was the best date she'd ever been on. Haruki was successful, handsome, and interesting. And he wasn't afraid of smart women or women who loved bugs. Izumi allowed herself a brief fantasy of a second date, an engagement, a wedding. She saw them on their honeymoon in a rain forest, tracking down exotic species.

But then, Haruki accidentally dropped his cloth napkin. Instead of calling the waiter for a new one, he leaned down to pick it up.

'Arghhhh!' He jerked back and pulled his feet up onto the banquet.

'What is it?' Izumi thought he was having a heart attack.

'Waiter!'

Some nearby diners looked over in alarm. The uniformed waiter rushed to their table. 'Yes, sir? How may I help you?'

With a trembling finger, Haruki pointed under the table. 'Th-there's a c-c-cockroach!'

Izumi sighed.

The following Monday, she sat at her desk and drew the handkerchief out of her purse. She used it to pat her hands dry after washing them, but the thin cotton was unabsorbent and so it wasn't even a particularly useful gift. It was simply pretty. She remembered a recent article about nuptial gifts. She grabbed the latest copy of *Insects of the World* and flipped through the pages till she found it. Ah, yes:

> In experiments reported this week, researchers Natasha LeBas and Leon Hockham from the University of St Andrews removed the valuable (i.e., edible) nuptial gift that male empidid dance flies normally provide their female partner and replaced the gift with either a large edible gift or an inedible cotton ball token that resembles tokens given by other empidid fly species. The researchers found that although pairs copulated longest after presentation of a large edible gift, the

> females receiving the worthless cotton ball token were sufficiently tricked to allow males to copulate for as long as when the males provided a small nutritious gift. Males who substitute highly visible, but easily obtainable and worthless gifts may thus be able to invade a population of genuine gift-giving males.
>
> The research demonstrates that, at least in some cases, females are susceptible to the invasion of so-called male cheating behaviour, and it suggests that the evolution of worthless gift-giving may arise though males' sensory exploitation of female preferences for nutritious gifts.

Izumi shuddered a little. She had almost been taken in like the female empidid dance fly. She had almost fallen for a piece of worthless cloth.

Her mother called. 'Izumi-chan, the poor man thinks you won't go out with him again because he took you to a dirty restaurant.'

'*Okaasan*, how can I think of marrying a man who is afraid of cockroaches?'

'Well . . .'

'Did you know, by the way, that a cockroach can survive for up to nine days without its head? Or that they have teeth in their stomach?'

'I'm about ready to give up on you,' her mother said. 'I guess I will never have any grandchildren. Our bloodline will disappear with you.'

'Here's another interesting fact. During the war in Vietnam, the US army used cockroaches to root out guerrillas. They sprinkled the guerrillas' hideouts with synthetic roach pheromones and then made suspects walk past cages in which there were male roaches. Then they watched to see how the insects reacted . . .'

'I'm hanging up now, Izumi. I hope you will consider giving that nice young man a second chance.'

Click.

She paced her office a few times, trying to dispel her irritation. A fly had somehow become trapped in her office and was now bumping against the window glass. She swiftly moved to set it free. The fly zoomed out, and the plaintive sound of insect legs rubbing together wound its way into the room. Or no, not an insect. A violin. The same foreign man she'd seen before was sitting on the bench in the courtyard, but this time he was wielding a bow.

Maybe I'll just go say hello, Izumi thought. The man seemed lonely. Perhaps he didn't have any friends.

She locked her office and trotted down the stairs. He looked up when she appeared. His eyes, behind the thick lenses of his glasses, were protuberant, but he had a nice smile and a head of thick dark curls. She felt something sizzle between them. Pheromones, no doubt.

'Hello. I'm Dr Izumi Tanaka, Professor of Entomology,' she said in English, holding out her hand.

'Greg Samsa.' His fingers closed around hers. 'I used to be in sales, but my passion lies in music.'

'Well then, perhaps you are familiar with Bartok's *Mikrokosmos*.' Izumi said.

'Yes! *From the Diary of a Fly* is one of my favourite piano pieces.'

Izumi's eyes widened. She moved to sit down beside him, slowly, so he wouldn't scare and scuttle away. 'You're not American . . .'

'No. I'm from Prague. I'm afraid I don't speak much Japanese.'

'Well, if you need someone to show you around . . .'

'Thank you.' He rested the violin on his knee. 'Actually, would you happen to know of any good climbing walls nearby?'

Her heartbeat quickened. 'I'll find one and let you know. Where can I reach you?'

They chatted a bit more, then she went back to her office to do a web search. She found several climbing walls within driving distance. If he didn't have a car, she would offer to drive him herself.

As it turned out, Greg had the use of an aging hatchback discarded by a fellow professor. He invited Izumi to join him and promised to pick her up at her apartment.

She dressed in sneakers and Lycra, thought about applying fake eyelashes, then decided not to. Greg seemed like someone who'd prefer the natural look. In the mirror, she noted that her cheeks were flushed, her pupils dilated. As a scientist, she understood that attraction was a chemical reaction. Desire was transformative.

A buzz indicated Greg's arrival. Izumi rushed to open the door.

'Hello,' he said. 'This is for you.' In the bowl of his hand was an apple.

'Oh!' She might have expected flowers or cake but not this. She picked it up by its stem, noted the small bruise at the bottom of the fruit, and brought it to her mouth. Her eyes sought out Greg's behind his glasses as her teeth punctured the peel. She didn't bother to wipe away the juice that ran down her chin. She imagined his tongue shooting out like a proboscis, licking the sweetness from her skin, but he didn't touch her. Not yet.

'Shall we go?'

Later, after she had marvelled at the way Greg moved from hold to hold, clinging to the wall as if his fingers had hooks, she made a pre-emptive call to her mother. 'I met someone,' she said.

'Oh, that's wonderful!'

Izumi could imagine her flapping her apron in delight.

'Tell me about him! Where is he from? What does he do?'

'Well, he's a professor,' Izumi began.

'That's perfect!' No doubt she was already planning the wedding and pondering names for grandchildren.

'And he's Czech.'

Her mother did not reply. She had not been prepared for a foreigner. Izumi suspected that she would eventually come around, however. She was desperate for her daughter to settle down. A Caucasian would be better than no man at all.

The next few months were a whirlwind of climbing and concerts. They went to movies (foreign, with subtitles) and had dinner in elegant restaurants. At night, Izumi dreamed of their limbs forming a heart in mid-air.

In mid-summer, when the semester had finally ended, Greg invited her to go on a picnic.

'I'll prepare rice balls,' Izumi promised in a rare moment of behaviour that her mother would deem gender appropriate.

'I'll bring the nectar,' Greg rejoined. 'Shall we take the tram?'

This is it, Izumi thought. He's going to ask me to marry him.

They met at the station. Izumi carried their lunch in a wrapping cloth. Greg had a backpack with a blanket and a bottle of wine tucked inside. When he saw her, he held out his hand. They stepped onto the tram together.

Izumi was hardly aware of the city as it flashed by. She ignored the other passengers, fixating on Greg instead. She couldn't help herself; the pheromones were so powerful.

The scent of diesel and garbage gave way to that of grass and cedar. The horizon was smudged with green. When they finally reached their stop, they descended into a field of wildflowers. A forest was just beyond. As they walked towards the trees, the flowers seemed to grow taller and taller until they were past Izumi's knees, past her waist, past her chest. She still gripped Greg's hand, but it felt different somehow. His fingers had narrowed and lengthened. When she turned to look at his face, she suddenly saw him as if through a kaleidoscope.

'Are you ready?' His voice when it came to her was not English or Japanese or any language that she'd known until now, but she understood him completely.

'Yes,' she replied.

She felt the tickle of grass on her toes and then her feet were no longer touching the ground. As she rose above her shoes, now as large as ships, now growing ever smaller, she reminded herself that desire is transformative. Catching a draft of air, she glided towards the sun. Greg was right beside her.

The Lump

When Lexie first noticed the soreness in her left armpit, she thought that it was due to a pulled muscle—maybe from carrying that heavy bag of kitty litter—but after a week, she started to get worried. She was quite sure that the area was swollen. She thought about barging in on Kentaro and asking him what he thought, but they weren't speaking. Or at least he wasn't speaking to her. He'd told her that he was practising living alone, that he was thinking about divorce. Their house was large enough, their schedules different enough, that they could go for days without seeing each other even though they were still sleeping under one roof—Lexie, in the master bedroom, Kentaro, in a smaller tatami room down the hall.

Lexie never knew for sure what exactly would set him off, but this time it had been because of the cats. She had noticed that Fifi, her fluffy black princess, was refusing to drink water from her stainless-steel bowl. She took an old plastic dish out of the cupboard, filled it with water, and set it on the floor.

'What are you doing?' Kentaro asked, his voice dripping with disdain. 'That's my bento box.'

'But you never use it,' Lexie said. 'And anyway, we can wash it.'

It didn't help that two minutes later, Fifi hopped up onto the kitchen table and started grooming herself.

Kentaro looked at Lexie. When she didn't react, he shouted 'Get off!' and Fifi scurried behind the sofa. 'Ugh. She was in the litter box just five minutes ago. It's like wearing toilet slippers on the table.'

Lexie thought of showing Kentaro Instagram photos of a certain fashion designer's cherished Persian eating from a silver dish placed beside her master's plate. And then there was that famous singer who also let his cat sit on the table while he himself dined, sometimes feeding his pet caviar from his own fork.

'They probably jump on the table and the counter all the time when we're gone, at work,' she said. 'And we've never gotten sick. The germs have probably helped us build up our immune systems.'

That was the last straw. Kentaro sputtered something about 'filthy animals' and 'different values', and she hadn't laid eyes on him since. Although he had been making breakfast for the two of them for the past three years, he suddenly started leaving the house early, before she got up, and coming home late, when she was already in bed. She figured he was stopping at convenience stores on the way to work for a rice ball and some coffee. Maybe afterwards, he went someplace cheap, like Yoshiya, for beef-on-rice, and then hung out in pachinko parlours. Meanwhile, Lexie spent every evening at home with a book, a glass of wine, and both cats sprawled across her legs. At bedtime, Fifi and

Prince, the tabby, followed her up the stairs and arranged themselves around her sleeping body.

Lexie had always known that Kentaro wasn't a cat person, but he had been the one to bring the animals into their lives. Every once in a while, he'd talked about getting a dog—maybe a poodle, like his mother had had, or one of those big affable Akita dogs (although the climate in Shikoku wasn't really suitable for a dog with such a thick coat). Lexie liked dogs and had fond memories of her childhood pets, but she hadn't been enthusiastic about getting one in adulthood. She knew that she would be the one who would have to walk it, feed it, and take it to the vet. Kentaro's working hours were longer than hers. She taught English part-time at area kindergartens and community centres. And then one day, Kentaro's high school friend had called him up and asked him if he wanted a couple of kittens. To Lexie's surprise, her husband said 'yes'.

Kentaro had been the one to buy and assemble the cat tree. He brought home scratching posts and toys, including mechanical birds that flew around the living room. He was the one who reached under the table at dinnertime with titbits of food. He'd even taken Fifi to the vet for her shots and later, to be spayed.

Gradually, however, he had become more and more exasperated with the cats, swatting them with newspapers when they clawed at the furniture and shoving them off of his lap when they dared to playfully bite his fingers. In an attempt to discipline Prince for hissing at him, he had held the cat immobile and yelled in his feline face, which hadn't made the tabby any more submissive or obedient or affectionate. The cats began to avoid him, preferring Lexie's soft touch and gentle voice. Now, he couldn't stand them. 'You behave as if you like the cats more than me,' he sneered when, upon hearing Prince meowing at the door, she jumped up to open it. 'Maybe you should decide who you'd rather live with—Prince and Fifi, or me.'

Now, Lexie sat on the sofa, which had been scarred with claw marks, with Fifi on her lap. Fifi was the more affectionate and needier of the two cats. Her purring soothed Lexie's frayed nerves. She buried her fingers in the cat's plush fur. Prince would tolerate a few rubs on his head before he would bite or reach out a claw, signalling that he'd had enough. Lexie still had a scratch from several days before. But she wasn't concerned about that. She was becoming obsessed with the lump.

She kept thinking of Kentaro's father, who had died from lung cancer. Although Kentaro's relationship with his dad had been contentious at best, he had spent many nights in the hospital at the man's bedside, wiping his brow and offering him sips of water. Lexie had walked in on them once to find Kentaro reading to him in a voice filled with tenderness. Of course, Lexie didn't want to be diagnosed with cancer, but if she were, maybe Kentaro would forget about their feud. Maybe he would turn into a gentle caretaker, bringing her turkey sandwiches and trashy American magazines as she sat propped against pillows. If she went bald from chemo, maybe he would shave his head in solidarity. She finally made a mammogram appointment at a local hospital.

Lexie thought about texting Kentaro. Maybe he would offer to go with her to the hospital. She even went so far as to type out a message on her phone but then quickly deleted it. What if it was nothing? Then she would be mocked for taking to desperate measures to earn his sympathy. No, it was better to wait until she had something concrete to convey.

In the meantime, she tried to better control the cats. Whenever Fifi jumped onto the counter, she turned on the faucet and flicked water at the cat until she jumped back down onto the floor, mewling indignantly. When Prince meowed at the door, she counted to ten before she let him come in or go out, thinking that he might learn to be more patient.

Every evening, she made a nice meal and set the table for two, on the off chance that Kentaro would come home in time for dinner. Every evening, she ate by herself, then scraped Kentaro's portion into the trash. She wouldn't be able to serve it the next day. He always complained when she served leftovers.

Before she left for her mammogram, she sat down on the scarred sofa and beckoned the cats with a pat. Fifi immediately bounded onto her lap and rubbed her head against Lexie's chin. Prince followed close behind and allowed Lexie to scratch between his ears a little longer than usual.

'Thanks, guys,' Lexie told them. 'You're the best.'

At the hospital, she had to fill out forms and show her insurance card.

'Do you have any special concerns?' the receptionist asked.

Lexie took a deep breath. 'I have a lump under my arm.'

The receptionist's brow furrowed. Lexie's heart began to canter. A few minutes later she was directed to the room with the dreaded mammogram machine. The last time she'd had her breasts examined, there had been an elderly white-haired physician who'd called her 'mother'. She had given no indication that she had children—and in fact did not have any, although she referred to herself as such when speaking to her cats. ('Mommy missed you so much,' she would say after coming home from the kindergarten and finding them waiting at the door.)

This time, the technician was a young woman with a ponytail, but she was no more gentle than the elderly male doctor had been as she positioned and compressed Lexie's breasts in the vise-like machine. Lexie endured the torture, then said, 'I have a lump.' In her experience, Japanese medical personnel didn't like to be told what they would find and became irritated when patients suggested their own diagnosis, but she wanted to make sure that whatever it was she had didn't go unnoticed.

'Where?' the young woman asked.

Lexie lifted her arm to show her. She invited the young woman to touch the swelling. 'Ah, yes, hmmm.'

See? She wasn't imagining it.

'You'll be seeing the doctor next,' the technician said. She laid her hand on Lexie's shoulder for just a moment—an unusual, consoling gesture in this land where people rarely touched one another.

Lexie put her bra and shirt back on, then went to another room where she was instructed to disrobe again. She went behind a pink curtain and put her clothes in a wicker basket. When she opened the curtain, she saw a woman doctor in a white coat.

'Hello,' the doctor said, in English. 'Lie down here, and I will do an ultrasound.'

Lexie did as she was told. The doctor smoothed gel over her breasts and then Lexie felt the cool wand passing over them. She couldn't bear to look at the screen.

'No problem,' the doctor said in a cheerful tone.

'But what about this swelling,' Lexie said, lifting up her arm.

The doctor probed with the wand. 'Yes, there's a bit of fluid there,' she confirmed. She pressed the spot with her fingers and bit her lip, thinking. 'Do you have a cat?'

'Umm, yes. Two.'

'Has one of your cats scratched you recently?'

Lexie remembered the gash from Prince on her wrist, which had been slow to heal. 'Uh, yes, actually . . .'

'It's possible that some bacteria has gotten into your body. I'll prescribe antibiotics. If it doesn't clear up, come back.' She chuckled then. 'It's been a long time since I have seen a case of Cat Scratch Fever.'

Lexie's shoulders loosened. She could just imagine what Kentaro would say. She knew that she would never mention this visit to him.

When she got home, as she stabbed her key into the lock, she could hear the cats yowling on the other side of the door. As soon as she stepped inside, their yowls turned to purrs. To celebrate her good news, she decided that she would pan grill a piece of salmon and serve it with a bowl of fluffy white rice and steamed broccoli. She'd make miso soup with cubes of tofu and chopped green onions. She took two wine glasses from the cabinet and poured herself a glass of wine. Then she thought better of it and put the other glass back onto the shelf.

Just as she was sitting down to eat her dinner, she heard Kentaro's car pull into the driveway. She froze. She heard the car door open and slam, his footsteps on the concrete steps, his key in the lock. Then she decided. She would ask him for a divorce.

With her chopsticks, she broke off a morsel of pink fleshed fish and set it on a napkin next to her plate. She looked down at Prince who sat at her feet. 'Here you go, boy,' she said, patting the table. He gazed back at her for a moment, perhaps disbelieving, and then with a swift, graceful motion, jumped onto the table and bent his head to devour the salmon.

Lexie didn't shoo him away.

Mon-chan

Nahoko had dropped in on her mother for her weekly visit. As they sat at the kitchen table drinking green tea and crunching rice crackers, she noticed that Okaasan had framed a photo of Marilyn Monroe on top of the television. How odd, especially since there weren't any photos of her grandchildren displayed in the room. But she knew what Marilyn meant to her mother.

Nahoko and her family had spent three years in Atlanta while her husband Jun was on overseas assignment. Whenever Nahoko had seen an image of Marilyn Monroe on a T-shirt or a poster or in a magazine over there, she'd thought of her mother. As a child, she'd loved to hear Okaasan talk about Marilyn or Mon-chan, as she had been known in Japan, once the biggest foreign box office draw in the country. She'd flown into Narita for her honeymoon with the famous baseball player, Joe DiMaggio. Nahoko's mother had been a teenager then, and she'd been at the airport with her three best friends when the Pan American jet landed. Mobs of reporters and fans crowded the tarmac, the policemen on security duty just barely holding them back.

Nahoko's mother had managed to snap a photo of the honeymooners as they got off the plane—Marilyn beaming in her fur, Joe looking dour at her side. The photo was a tad blurry and a bit faded by now, but Nahoko had always figured it was worth some money. People were auctioning sales receipts and ashtrays left behind by famous people on eBay. If her mother wanted, she could sell it. But the one time her daughter had suggested such a thing, she had scoffed.

'This is my best memory,' she'd said. 'I'd never trade it for money.'

A memory better than her own wedding day and honeymoon? Nahoko wondered. *Better than the day she became a mother?* Although losing out to five minutes of Marilyn was wounding, Nahoko reminded herself that her mother was no longer as sensible and logical as she'd once been. It wasn't altogether surprising that Nahoko's mother brought up Mon-chan now more than ever.

'Right after I took that photo, those two got right back on the plane,' she said, nodding towards the TV. She picked up her tea cup and slurped loudly. 'There were so many people crowded around that they couldn't get through, so they slipped out the baggage hatch.'

Nahoko nodded, feigning interest, although she'd memorized these facts long ago.

'Joe bought her a string of Mikimoto pearls,' she went on. 'And they stayed at the Imperial Hotel.'

As a girl, Nahoko's mother had saved newspaper and magazine photos of Marilyn and Joe strolling along the lawns of the Kawana Hotel, another photo of them dining at the Royal Host, a chain restaurant specializing in Hawaiian home-cooking. The album also contained a clipping of Marilyn singing to the troops in Korea. It had been February, mid-winter, and there was snow in the air, but Marilyn had skipped out on her honeymoon to appear before 100,000 American soldiers in a flimsy purple sequined dress.

'She sang, "Diamonds are a Girl's Best Friend".' Nahoko's mother proceeded to hum a few bars. At one time, she had known all the words—in English, no less.

'"The Honourable Buttocks-Swinging Actress,"' she quoted from a long-ago news report, and giggled. 'When she came back from Korea, she had a fever of 104 and a touch of pneumonia. Joe had to nurse her back to health before they could continue their honeymoon.'

Nahoko had read that Joe DiMaggio had been abusive to Marilyn, but for her mother, he remained saintly, a perfect gentlemen. He left roses on Marilyn's grave until he died! Nahoko's father had never bothered to tend to his wife when she'd been in bed with the flu. It had always been Nahoko, or her older sister, Mariko.

According to tradition, Mariko was the one responsible for their mother now. Or Mariko's husband, rather. The plan was that Mariko would find a nice guy with a good job, get married, and he'd become the eldest son. Their father had been adopted, too, changing his name when he entered the family. But Mariko wasn't all that interested in marriage. As soon as she'd finished high school, she'd fled to Tokyo. She'd studied design with hip city kids, shaking off all of her old-fashioned small-town values in four years. As she'd told Nahoko many times, she was never going back.

'But what about when Okaasan is old? What if she can't take care of herself?' Nahoko had asked after their father died. By this time, she had a family of her own—a boy, Satoshi, and a girl, Momoe, and, of course, her husband, Jun. She'd made a point of marrying a second-born son so she wouldn't have to live with her in-laws.

'We'll cross that bridge when we come to it,' Mariko had said. 'She's still young.'

'Did your husband take care of you when you were sick in America?' Her mother asked now, memories of Joe DiMaggio somehow triggering thoughts of Jun.

Of course not! No matter where he was, he was too preoccupied to notice or care. But she didn't say this. 'I never got sick in Atlanta,' she lied.

Now, she was back in her hometown, back in their house. Her husband was living in Tokyo, where he had been transferred after their return to Japan. They hadn't wanted to uproot their children again, so Nahoko had stayed behind. It had been over a month since she'd seen Jun. He came home once in a while but more often than not, he spent weekends working in Tokyo. Although in Atlanta, they'd eaten dinner together almost every night, once back in Japan he'd been reclaimed by Japanese corporate culture and reverted to his former busy, remote self.

Just as her mother poured more tea in her cup, her cell phone buzzed. She checked the screen. It was her daughter's homeroom teacher. The week before, she'd called to complain about the magenta streaks in Momoe's hair. What was it this time?

'Moshi moshi?'

'Were you aware that Momoe did not come to school today?'

Nahoko sighed. 'No, I was not.'

Jun called that evening.

'I think our daughter has fallen in with a bad crowd.' Nahoko twisted the hem of her nightgown in her fist as she spoke, feeling ashamed because she couldn't keep the kids in control, the household in order.

Her husband merely grunted on the other end.

'Did you hear me?' She felt a flash of irritation. 'Her homeroom teacher called me this morning. She said that Momoe has been missing classes. Sometimes she doesn't show up at all.'

'What do you want me to do?' She could hear him sigh over the wires. 'Should I come home? Do you want me to talk to her?'

Yes, she wanted to say. But she could read the sarcasm in his tone. He was preparing for a business trip to China to launch a new product, and he couldn't possibly return to Tokushima that weekend or the next. And, quite frankly, he didn't know how to talk to teenagers. These were rhetorical questions. It was her job to manage the home front, while he made the money that supported their comfortable lifestyle.

'How's Satoshi?' he asked. 'How's the baseball?'

Typical. Change the subject. And yet, he had a right to ask about his son, and she was grateful for his interest.

'He's fine. You should see him. He oils his baseball glove every night before he goes to sleep, just like Ichiro. He's really good, you know. There's a tournament coming up in July. If you could come down for even one game, he'd be so happy.' She was babbling, trying to fit as many words in as possible before he lost interest.

'I'll think about it. Is he studying?'

'Yes,' she assured him. 'He's getting great marks in English and his math is improving.' Why did she have to work so hard to sell these children to their father? Why couldn't he just ask them himself?

'And your mother?'

Nahoko paused for a few beats. She knew that Jun wasn't overly fond of her mother. He thought she was silly and hysterical. His own mother was an ice queen.

'One of her neighbours called me,' she said slowly. 'She's been digging holes in her yard and burying things. She thinks someone has been stealing her dishes.'

From Tokyo, only silence.

'I've been thinking she should move in with us for a while. She needs company. Her doctor says that she's losing her grip on reality.'

He knew about responsibility. He could hardly deny her this, and yet, even as she waited for his consent, she knew she was giving him yet another excuse to stay away.

He sighed again. 'As you wish.'

While they'd been living in Atlanta, Nahoko had worried about her children's education. Sure, their English improved—after three years abroad, they spoke better than she did; she couldn't understand them when they were talking to their American friends—but their Japanese skills had deteriorated. She'd sent them to Japanese school on Saturdays at first, but Satoshi had wanted to play baseball, and Momoe pleaded that she wanted to go to so-and-so's pool party, or to the mall with somebody else, and finally she'd given up. When in Rome . . . Her husband had insisted that they keep up with their kanji. Nahoko had ordered workbooks by mail from Japan, and every now and then she'd asked if they'd done their homework, but she hadn't pressured them too much. Like her kids, she'd been seduced by the relaxed, anything-goes atmosphere, the freedom of America. She'd let them eat cornflakes for breakfast and sandwiches for lunch.

But now, she understood that she had been wrong. If Satoshi and Momoe were going to succeed in their native country, they needed discipline. They needed a thousand kanji to read the newspaper. They needed to blend in with their peers. And she needed to be a better mother. And daughter.

In spite of her resolve, she missed the following Monday's visit. Two weeks later, she got a phone call from one of her mother's neighbours.

'I think you'd better check in with your mother,' the woman said. 'She's had her locks changed two days in a row. She seems confused.'

'Busybody!' Nahoko muttered to herself after hanging up the phone. And yet, she felt guilty. For the past three years, she'd been relieved to be on the other side of the globe from her mother, too far away to be at her beck and call. Her sister had been in Japan—in Tokyo, but at least she was in the same time zone. Their mother could call her and rant about the neighbours without worrying about the time difference. Now that Nahoko was back in the same prefecture, just twenty minutes away by car, her mother had started calling daily, on the slightest pretext. For the most part, she tried to pre-empt these calls, phoning her as soon as the kids had gotten off to school. But sometimes Okaasan forgot that they had spoken and called again a few hours later, wondering why she hadn't heard from her youngest daughter.

Nahoko took her time getting ready. She put on make-up—it was rude not to—and cut some daffodils from the little garden she'd started at the side of the house. She wrapped them in a cone of newspaper and set out for her mother's house.

When she got there, she found that the door was locked. She rang the bell. As she waited, she gazed around the yard, noting the weeds that had grown up on the pebble path leading to the door. Her mother had always been so meticulous, weeding and sweeping the concrete driveway almost daily. From inside, she heard the sound of footsteps. The door opened just a crack.

'Who is it?'

'Okaasan, it's me. Nahoko.'

The door opened wider.

Nahoko breathed in sharply. Her mother's hair was all snarly as if it hadn't been combed all week. The air, when she stepped inside the dimmed room, was stale, slightly putrid. Obviously the windows hadn't been opened in days.

'Mother, are you okay? Have you been sick?'

'I'm fine,' she said. She grabbed Nahoko's sleeve and dragged her towards the kitchen. 'I have to show you something.' She opened the refrigerator. The shelves were laden with small unwrapped dishes of mouldy leftovers. Bowls of rice covered in bluish fuzz. Egg salad that had turned green. 'Look here. Someone has been putting rotten food inside.'

It was still morning, but Nahoko felt a wave of fatigue coming on. 'Mother, I think you must have put this stuff in here and forgotten about it.'

'I would never do such a thing.' She looked at her daughter and gave a little cry. 'You did it, didn't you? It was you!'

With a sinking heart, Nahoko realized that nothing she said at that moment would make any difference.

Later, at home, she realized she would have to call Mariko. Just the thought of her sister filled her with exasperation—and maybe a little envy. In Tokyo, her sister was oblivious to their mother's decline. She had no idea that Okaasan's refrigerator was filled with rotting food, that she'd padlocked all her cupboards shut and lost most of the keys, that she was convinced someone, a prowler, was creeping into her room every night and touching her feet. But Mariko needed to know these things. Nahoko sighed deeply and picked up the phone.

Since it was a weekday afternoon, she knew that Mariko would be at work, awake and sober. Sometimes when she called her sister on her cell phone, she could hear music in the background or trains or voices. It was hard to talk if she knew that Mariko was at a party or using public transportation. But if she was at her desk, at least she would be still.

The phone rang once, twice, and then, 'Sis! What's happening?'

'Mariko, it's about Okaasan. She's not doing so well. I think she has Alzheimer's or something.'

'I just talked to her yesterday,' Mariko said. 'She sounded fine to me. We got into this long conversation about that white dress that Marilyn Monroe wore while standing over the grating. Do you remember? That famous photo of Marilyn trying to hide her underwear?'

'I'm serious, Mariko. Last week when I went to visit her at three o'clock in the afternoon she was still wearing her nightclothes.' She'd seemed disoriented. When Nahoko had pointed to the clock, she'd cried out in surprise. In childhood, their mother had gotten up before anyone else in the household, and she'd always been dressed when the girls stumbled into the kitchen for breakfast.

'Ha! Pajamas at three o'clock. That sounds like me!' Mariko's hand went over the receiver for a moment, and Nahoko could hear her speaking to someone else, a co-worker perhaps.

When she came back on, Nahoko said, 'Yeah, well, Okaasan isn't out in Roppongi until the wee hours of the morning. She goes to bed at about eight, in case you forgot.'

Mariko sighed into the phone. 'Listen, sis. Work is busy right now. We're heavily into the fall collection and I can't get away. I'll send her a robot.'

'A robot? What are you talking about?'

The line went dead. Nahoko threw her cell phone across the room. It cracked, and yet minutes later, it began to ring.

A package was delivered to her mother a week later. As soon as it arrived, Okaasan called, wanting help.

'I can't get this box opened,' she fussed. 'I think it must be locked.'

Nahoko sighed. She was in the middle of making pickles. She couldn't just get up and leave. 'What box?'

'From your sister Mariko,' she said. 'A present from Tokyo.' Her voice was filled with impatience, like a kid held back from the booty on Christmas morning. 'When can you get here?' she whined.

If Nahoko waited until the next morning, her mother would probably call several more times that day. She'd forget that she'd already made the request. Or maybe she just did it to spite her daughter. 'Give me an hour,' she said, surrendering another afternoon to her mother's 'emergency'.

When she arrived, she found that Okaasan had managed to peel off the brown wrapping paper to reveal a large box. There was a picture of a fluffy white stuffed seal—no, a robot—on the side of the box. So this is what Mariko had been talking about—the latest rage, therapeutic robotic animals meant to comfort the sick and elderly.

Nahoko wondered if it would work, if it would keep her mother company and distract her enough so that she would stop calling ten times a day. She went into the kitchen and got a knife and then she opened up the box. She showed her mother how to charge the robot, using an adapter that went into the seal's mouth like a pacifier.

'So soft,' her mother said, stroking the fur. And then she made cooing sounds, the same sounds that she used to make with the little Pomeranian they'd once had.

Nahoko sighed. At best, it would buy her some time. Clearly, a robot seal was a stop-gap measure, something that might slow down her mother's dementia, if they were lucky. But Nahoko suspected it was too late.

'Do you want to give it a name?' Nahoko asked.

Her mother clasped her hands together, suddenly girlish. 'I think I'll call her Mon-chan,' she said. 'After Marilyn Monroe.'

When it was finally all juiced up, the baby seal began to move her head. She let out a small yelp, as if she were seeking her mother. Her flippers flapped like wings.

'Here I am, my darling Mon-chan,' the elderly woman said. 'I'm right here.'

It's just a stupid toy! Nahoko thought. Filled with a sudden, aimless fury, she scooped the seal robot into her arms and held it, away from her mother's grasping hands. The thing kept moving, as if trying to squirm out of her grip, but she held on tightly, burying her face in its fur.

Peace on Earth

According to the Prime Minister, Japan and the United States are best friends. So why are my parents always arguing?

Just this morning, my father made breakfast—ojiya, which is miso soup mixed with leftover rice and an egg. He said, 'Isn't this better than hotcakes? All that sugar?'

Mom had made blueberry pancakes yesterday. She didn't say anything, but sighed loudly, and then looked longingly towards the row of breakfast cereals on the kitchen counter.

'Taiga-kun, what do you think?' Otosan said, looking at me.

I shrugged. I'll eat anything and I like both kinds of breakfast—Mom's American ones and Otosan's Japanese ones—but since he got started on this cooking kick, it seems like every meal is part of a competition between them. My sister, Maya, and I looked at each other across the table and rolled our eyes.

'Did you hear them last night?' Maya asked me later, as we rode our bikes to school.

'How could I not? *Urusakatta, na.*'

They'd been watching some DVD about World War II, and Otosan started going on about the atomic bomb. Then Mom jumped in and their voices got louder and louder.

'I think you should apologize to Ueno-san,' Maya said, making her voice lower like Otosan's.

Mrs Ueno is our elderly next-door neighbour. She was in Nagasaki at the time of the bomb. She's pretty cheerful, but her voice is a little strange—high and squeaky. Otosan says it's because of radiation poisoning.

'Why do you always hold me responsible?' I imitate Mom. 'I didn't drop that bomb. I would have been opposed to it, if I'd been alive then. I married you, didn't I? Doesn't that prove anything?'

Maya laughs, but then she gets serious. 'What do you think other parents fight about?'

I shrug, letting go of the handlebar for a second. 'Which professional baseball team is the best?'

'Or maybe whose turn it is to take out the trash?' Maya guesses.

'Maybe if Mom and Otosan were from the same country, they'd always get along.'

'So, kanna?'—maybe.

That evening, the argument is about where to go for a winter vacation. Mom wants to go back to the States to visit her family—Grandma and Grandpa, Aunt Ann and Uncle Brad, my cousins.

'We haven't seen them in almost two years,' she says.

'We need to save money,' Otosan says. 'It's too expensive to go all the way to Wisconsin, but we could take a trip somewhere closer to home. Any ideas, kids?'

Me, I don't care where we go or if we go or not. I'd be happy just to sleep in every day and hang out at the batting centre with my friends. Or maybe I could get Chiaki, this girl in my homeroom, to go to karaoke with me.

'Hawaii?' Maya says. I guess it's because she loves watching our parents' wedding video. They got married on a plantation on Oahu, with a waterfall trickling down rocks and leis around their necks. They look really happy in that video. They're not fighting. Instead, they're feeding each other coconut wedding cake, dancing, and kissing.

'Hmmm.' Otosan rubs his forehead.

'Why don't we go to Okinawa?' I suggest. Because of the army base, I know that there are lots of Americans there. Mom might feel sort of at home. And with all the palm trees and sugar cane fields, it's probably sort of like Hawaii.

'Okinawa,' Otosan repeats, letting the idea sink in. He's a high school teacher, and he's been down there on school trips. The students at the school Maya and I attend usually go north to Hokkaido for skiing, so we've never been to Naha.

'Okinawa!' Mom says. 'I've always wanted to go there!'

Mom likes to travel. Before she met Otosan, she'd been to half a dozen countries in Europe. She'd planned on spending a year or two teaching English in Japan before going to Thailand, India, and various places in Africa. But she got stuck here, she says. She met Otosan and fell in love, and then she couldn't leave. So now she only gets to go someplace if we all go together.

She has her bags packed a week before we're scheduled to leave. I wait until the last minute, then jam a couple pairs of shorts, some T-shirts, boxers, my baseball mitt, and a couple of comic books into my backpack. Oh, and a bathing suit. Mom says it'll be too cold for swimming in the ocean—the main reason most people from other parts of Japan go to Okinawa—but that our hotel has an indoor pool.

I'm looking forward to going to Okinawa because it's home to the National High School baseball champion. Last summer, I watched every game they played, and I'm hoping that something in the air down there will rub off on me and turn me into a pitcher as amazing as their ace, Shimabukuro. Maybe the island food will make me stronger—all that bitter melon and ham.

On the plane, Mom thumbs through her guidebook. 'Ooh,' she says. 'A&W! They have root beer in Okinawa!'

'What's A&W?' Maya asks.

'It's an American restaurant chain. I worked at one when I was in high school. Wow, it's been a long time . . .'

'What's root beer?' I ask. I'm too young to drink alcohol, so it's not like I'll get to try it.

'It's a soft drink. Like cola, but different. We'll have to try root beer floats! At A&W there's a bell at the entrance. If you're happy with the service, you ring the bell when you leave.'

And then wouldn't everybody be looking at you? How embarrassing would that be? I hope she doesn't go ringing the bell in Okinawa.

'We should go to the base too,' Otosan says, 'so you can see for yourself how noisy those planes are.'

My shoulders tense. When I came up with this plan, I must have forgotten. Whether or not the US military should be in Okinawa is the theme of another one of their arguments.

When an American army guy in Japan got into trouble, it made national news, and Otosan said, 'Why won't the Americans get out of Okinawa? We can defend ourselves.'

Then Mom said, 'When you use that tone, it sounds like you despise Americans. The kids are going to feel negative about their American-ness when they hear you talk like that.'

Luckily, Mom doesn't seem to hear him this time. Her nose is still buried in the guidebook.

'The snake museum!' she says, flipping eagerly through the pages. 'Live music!'

When we get off the plane in Naha, the wind is soft and warm. *So this is the tropics. Nice!* It's not cold, like home on Shikoku, where we can see our breath in the hallway. I immediately take off my jacket.

We gather our luggage and then take a bus to the car rental service, where Mom chews out Otosan for not having reserved a larger car. 'How are we supposed to jam all our stuff in here?' she asks. 'Somebody's going to have to ride on the roof!'

'Well, you shouldn't have brought along the Christmas presents,' he says. 'We could have opened those when we got back home.'

Somehow, we manage to cram everything in. With bags wedged between Maya and me up to the ceiling, there's no room in the backseat to move around.

The rest of the day is a blur of sightseeing. First, we hit up a red castle, once headquarters of the Ryukyu kingdom. We go through rooms filled with lacquered thrones and old scrolls. Whenever one of us falls behind, Otosan hurries us along. 'C'mon, c'mon!' he says. 'We only have three days in Okinawa, and we still have a lot to see!'

'Take it easy,' Mom grumbles back. 'This is vacation, not a packaged group tour.'

My stomach is growling by the time we get out of that place, but it's still an hour or so till lunch. Luckily, our next stop is Pineapple Park, where along with a pineapple grove and exhibits on pineapple cultivation and a little train shaped like a pineapple, there's a snack bar. Before Otosan can say anything about the harmful effects of sugar, I order a tropical fruit parfait with my own money.

Later, on the way to our hotel, we stop by the American Air Force base in Kadena. From the side of the road, we can see the rows of lookalike houses, all modest one-storey structures. They're nothing like the houses you see in American movies. They're not even as nice as the house where my grandparents live. There aren't any people milling about either. The place is pretty subdued.

'It looks peaceful,' Maya says. '*Shizuka na.*'

Otosan lowers the car window, but we hear no planes. The sky is clear, except for a few puffs of white, and quiet.

'Huh.' Otosan is clearly disappointed. 'When we brought our students here on the school trip it was very noisy.'

Mom shrugs. 'They're probably on winter vacation too.'

Otosan starts up the car again and drives off down the highway.

Once we're checked in at our hotel, we finally get a chance to relax. In our room, there's a little tray of plastic-wrapped cookies—*chinsuko*. I'm starving again, so when nobody's looking, I scarf them down. Maybe housekeeping will bring more if we ask.

Otosan's tired from all that driving. 'I'm going to take a nap before dinner,' he says. 'And don't forget, kids. We're signed up for glass-blowing at 7 p.m.'

So that means we've got about thirty minutes of free time. I noticed when we came in that there's a game room on the first floor. 'Hey, Maya, wanna go play some air hockey?'

'Okay.' She follows me to the elevator and down to the game room.

We go past the lobby, where a woman in an evening gown and Santa hat is singing Christmas carols. Her voice rises to the ceiling: 'Let there be peace on earth . . .'

Peace—that would be nice.

Maya, the mind reader, says, 'I wish they'd stop arguing.'

'Yeah, me too.'

The game room is empty. We've got it all to ourselves. We take our places at the air hockey table and I shove the puck her way.

Maya deflects my goal shot. 'Do you think they'll get divorced?'

I sometimes wonder this myself, and it worries me. If they split up, would we have to choose between them? And if we chose Mom, would she try to make us move to

America? Sure, we're half-American, but we've never lived in the States. Who would we hang out with? How would we know if something was cool or not? And we don't even know the words to the national anthem. Not only that, but Japan is my home. And I'm the starting pitcher on my high school's baseball team. They'd never make it to the tournament final without me. But since I'm the older brother, I think it's best to keep my mouth shut.

'Nah,' I say. 'They've always been like that, haven't they? They're used to each other now. If they were going to get divorced, they would have split up long ago.'

The following day, which happens to be the day before Christmas, we wake up early. Mom says something about needing coffee, but Otosan insists upon the Japanese breakfast buffet. I pile my plate with bitter melon fried with ham and eggs and eat three bowls of rice, washed down with guava tea. Then we're off to a famous aquarium about an hour from our hotel. We make it through in record time, and then have lunch.

'Where are we going now?' Maya asks, over a bowl of Chinese noodles.

'Himeyuri-kan,' Otosan says. 'It's an important historical site.' He glances over at Mom. 'It was a hospital during World War II.'

Mom presses her lips together, but she doesn't object. Maybe the lack of coffee is doing her in. Or maybe she's actually interested in visiting this place.

Otosan parks in a gravel lot next to a tour bus. We haul ourselves out of the car, past a souvenir shop with brightly printed shirts on sale, and up some stone steps. A group of high school students in uniform is hovering near some sort of shrine. Some people are praying, others are laying flowers and wreaths of origami cranes on the altar.

Otosan saunters ahead, then calls us over.

'Look at this, kids,' he says. He's leaning against a railing, pointing down a big hole.

'It looks like a tunnel,' I say.

'Yes. This was the entrance to the cave. To the *hospital.*'

Of course there is another entrance, now. We go through glass doors into an air-conditioned lobby where Otosan buys our tickets. And then we forge ahead, down the dark hallways that make up the museum. Along the walls there are exhibits. Photos. Artifacts: a dented canteen; pages torn out of a diary; primitive-looking medical tools. *Imagine having your leg cut off with a hack saw! And no anaesthesia!*

Eventually, we make our way to the main chamber. It's cool and dark. Before it was just a cave, damp rocks, maybe with some spider webs or bats hanging in the corner. But it's been fixed up nice. The walls are covered with black and white portraits. I look at the captions underneath: names, ages. Keiko Yamaguchi, fifteen years old, third year, First Girls' High School. Noriko Saito, fifteen years old, first year, Normal School. And on and on. There's one that reminds me of Chiaki from homeroom. Their eyes are kind of the same.

'Fifteen,' my sister whispers. 'Like us.' She leans against me as if she needs some comfort.

'Yeah.' My mouth goes dry. 'If we were living here back then, I wouldn't be playing baseball.'

'You'd be a soldier,' she says.

I try to imagine holding a rifle against my shoulder instead of a bat, war planes zooming by overhead, bombs dropping all around. And Maya with a roll of bandages or running around with bedpans and burying the dead. 'You'd be a nurse.'

I look away from the faces for a moment, turn back behind me, and spot Mom. She's reading something out of a big book on a stand at the centre of the room. Maya and I go over to check it out. The books are filled with stories written by the survivors. Testimonies.

I skim over some of the titles: 'A patient with no legs crawling in the mud.' 'Bloated corpses as large as gasoline drum cans.' 'I could hear maggots eating rotting flesh.'

I read about how the nurses were warned that if they revealed themselves, they would be raped and killed. So when the US Army guys called for them to come out of the cave, they didn't move. They thought it was a trick to lure them to their destruction. Most of the nurses stayed down in the cave. When the American soldiers gassed the cave, many of them were killed.

I read a few sentences out loud. 'It was so quiet you could hear a pin drop. So when you no longer heard someone's voice, you knew she was dead. One voice after another disappeared. First, Chinen-san, then Hamamoto-san, Ishikawa-san, Kanda-san, and Higa-san.'

I imagine this cave filled with bodies—some dead, some dying, some just barely hanging on. I imagine the stench of rotting limbs. Those girls must have been hungry and lonely and scared. They must have thought the world was coming to an end.

Mom puts a hand on my shoulder. She puts her arm around Maya's waist. And then I feel another, heavier hand drop down on my other shoulder. I turn to see Otosan standing behind us, his arms around our whole family, as if he's trying to keep us safe.

'It was a terrible thing,' Mom says, her voice all choked up.

We look at the portraits again, all those young faces.

By the time we emerge from the cave, back into the light, we are all sniffling and struggling to swallow the lumps in our throats. Just before we go out the door, we come across a guestbook, a place to write about how we feel.

Maya goes first. She grabs the pen and scribbles a whole page, like she's writing a letter to someone. Then she wipes her eyes, turns to a clean page, and hands the pen to me.

I grab it from her and stare at the blank page for a long time. What should I write? I don't even know how to describe all these weird emotions going through my body. I feel a little bit guilty at having such an easy life. And sad, of course. And angry at the Americans who gassed the cave and the Japanese who told the nurses to stay down there. I'm feeling too many things at once, and there's not really enough time to process them, so I just write, 'I'm sorry.'

An elderly Japanese lady leans on her cane near the entrance. She thanks us for coming—Mom, Maya, Otosan, and me. I think she must have been one of the nurses, but even if she was, she doesn't seem to harbour any bad feelings towards Americans or Japanese who married Americans or half-and-half kids, like me and Maya. She smiles at us as we go out the door.

This time when we go by the shrine, Mom stops and buys a flower. She lays it on the altar and puts her hands together in prayer. Then all of us go back to the car. I walk slowly, silently, my head bent down.

As we drive back to the hotel, we're each in our private worlds. I look out the window at the fields of sugar cane, the ocean in the distance, but what I'm really seeing is all those sad, dark eyes peering down from the cave walls. That girl who looked like Chiaki.

And then we go by a shop window that's all lit up with coloured lights and I remember that it's Christmas Eve. It doesn't seem like the right time to be all gloomy. I'm glad that I saw all those girls on the wall, and I know that I will never forget, but right now we need to cheer up.

An orange and brown sign that I recognize from the guidebook looms into view. As if on cue, my stomach growls.

'Hey, Otosan,' I say. 'Why don't we stop at A&W for supper?'

I expect some resistance, but he pulls into the parking lot without comment. For once, he doesn't have anything nasty to say about Americans and their dominance of Okinawa and the evils of sugar.

We go up to the counter and order burgers and root beer floats. Then we settle at a table near the window.

A root beer float, I discover, is a scoop of vanilla ice cream bobbing in brown bubbles. It's fizzy and creamy at the same time. It tastes a little different from anything I've ever had before, but it's delicious.

Otosan seems to think so too. He takes a sip and says, 'Mmmm.' And then Mom is humming along with him.

For once, they are in tune with each other. I know that it won't last. Eventually they'll start bickering again. But for now, we can enjoy this sweet peace.

When we're done eating, we head slowly back to the car. We look around for Mom, expecting to find her right behind us, but she's not. And then we hear the bell clanging at the entrance. She's there, a huge smile spread across her face, ringing that bell and ringing it again. Dad can't help but grin.

Acknowledgements

First, I would like to thank the editors of the journals and magazines where some of these stories first appeared sometimes in slightly different form:

'Day Pass' in *The Distillery*; 'France' in *Half Tones to Jubilee*; 'Blue Murder' as 'Birds in the Trees' in *Snowy Egret*; 'River of Dolls', 'Lessons', and 'The Snow Woman' in *Wingspan*, 'Down the Mountain' in *Pleaides*; 'A Real Job' in *poemmemoirstory*, 'Julia in the Desert' in *The Font*, 'The Lump' in *Fall Lines*, and 'The Woman Who Loved Insects' in *Transnational Literature*. I'd also like to thank Kitaab publisher, Zafar Anjum, and Monideepa Sahu for including 'Mon-chan' in *The Best Asian Short Stories 2017* anthology. 'Peace on Earth' was originally published in the collection *Tomo: Friendship through Fiction: An Anthology of Japan Teen Stories* (Stone Bridge Press, 2012) edited by Holly Thompson. In addition, I am deeply grateful to Nora Nazarene Abu Bakar for taking a chance on this collection and to Cassandra Chia for her excellent editorial suggestions, Surina Jain for her eagle eye, Divya Gaur for the stunning cover design, and everyone else at Penguin Random House SEA involved with the book. Thanks also to Helene Dunbar, Wendy Jones Nakanishi, Meredith Stephens, Susan Balogh, Mitali Chakravarty, and Kathy L. Murphy for feedback, support, and encouragement. Finally, my family has supported me throughout my writing career. I owe much gratitude to my parents, Alvin and Patricia Borsum, my sister-in-law, Kavita Borsum, my husband, Yukiyoshi Kamata, and my children, Jio and Lilia.